The Strange Case of
Dr Simmonds
& Dr Glas

Novels by the same author:

Ash on a Young Man's Sleeve
Some Corner of an English Field
O Jones, O Jones
There Was a Young Man from Cardiff

The Strange Case of

Dr Simmonds
& Dr Glas

DANNIE ABSE

ROBSON
BOOKS

First published in Great Britain in 2002 by Robson Books,
64 Brewery Road, London N7 9NY

A member of **Chrysalis** Books plc

British Library Cataloguing in Publication Data
A catalogue record for this title is available from the British
Library.

ISBN 1 86105 504

Typeset by FiSH Books, London WC1
Printed by Mackays of Chatham, Kent

PART ONE

F AILED AT LUNCH. I had quit Goodge Street station, walked up Charlotte Street to the White Tower full of hope. I left feeling defeated. 'I'm too old,' I thought. 'Duffy is of a different generation.'

I wish now that I had not blabbered on complacently about Carl Jung's notorious pre-war judgements, how he had once nauseously suggested that the SS men in Hitler's Germany were being transformed into a noble caste of knights ruling sixty million natives.

I should have put an imperious full-stop to my own over-anxious remarks and tactfully changed the subject when I discerned across the table Patrick Duffy's eyes go dull and humourless. Still, stupidly, I had blundered on: 'In 1936 Jung believed that there were two types of dictators – the chieftain type and the medicine-man type. He reckoned Hitler belonged to the latter category, the mouthpiece of the old gods, the Sibyl, the Delphic oracle.'

Patrick Duffy replaced his knife and fork on his plate with

some conspicuous deliberation before he replied quietly that Carl Jung had judged Adolf Hitler to be a psychic scarecrow.

'A psychic scarecrow,' he repeated.

'Yes,' I said, 'Jung certainly changed his tune after the defeat of Germany.'

I should have guessed much earlier that Duffy was a committed Jungian. He had talked enthusiastically about a book his firm was about to publish called *The Devil in Synchronicity*.

'Our author,' Duffy had pontificated, 'refers to many authenticated stories, for instance, of clocks that stop precisely at the moment of their owner's death. Like that pendulum clock in the palace of Frederick the Great at Sans Souci which stopped when the Emperor died.'

Though the rest of our conversation resumed politely, in halcyon enough tones, I could not recover to any degree that sense of friendliness evident when we had first sat down to dine.

'When exactly did you cease working for Drew and Davidson?' Duffy asked me.

'Eight years ago now. When they were taken over.'

'They're a very good literary agency. As a matter of fact they sold me *The Devil in Synchronicity*. I think it'll do very well.'

After he had called for the bill Patrick Duffy did promise to let me have the odd book to report on; but I doubt if much will come my way from him. I think he is the sort of person who believes in omens and takes cognisance of the astrology predictions in the tabloids. The people in publishing these days are not what they used to be.

I arrived home to discover my wife out shopping. She had left a note to say as much near the telephone. It was mid-afternoon already. I had a few books to read, first novels. (I still scout for one American publisher though they rarely take notice of my recommendations.) I felt extremely lazy though and it seemed an effort even to press the button on the answer phone.

The emotionless educated robot telephone voice pronounced, like an accusation, *You have three messages*. It was the third message that perplexed me. 'This is Yvonne Bloomberg. I want you...well...would you please...I think I should like you to call on me here. Would you do that? Sorry...I mean the most convenient time would be around about, say, four o'clock. Come for tea. Any weekday afternoon. I want to show you the journals. They are shocking, shocking...' The phone honoured silence for a few seconds before this Yvonne Bloomberg spelt out a Belsize Park address.

Yvonne Bloomberg? I did not know anyone of that name. What journals? Whose journals? Obviously not those of Yvonne Bloomberg, for who would find their own journals shocking? Was she an editor working for a publisher? Why should she want me to read the manuscript if she had already done so herself? Besides, in my retirement, as the years pass, publishers contact me less and less. The editors I used to deal with have themselves retired or been given their cards. It is some time now since the name Peter Dawson was known even within the incestuous publishing world. Perhaps Yvonne Bloomberg had simply dialled the wrong number, our number, by mistake?

Just then I heard the key turn in the front door lock so I returned to the hall. My wife entered, burdened with shopping. She had bought the whole of Sainsbury's from the look of it.

'Do you know anyone called Yvonne Bloomberg?' I asked.

'Give me a hand,' she said.

'You don't know an Yvonne Bloomberg, do you?' I persisted.

'No, I don't. Could you put these in the fridge?'

After traipsing back and forward from the front door to the kitchen (why does my dear wife get tempted so frequently to buy items we don't need or things we are forced to eat lest they go out of date and are wasted?) I was asked, 'How did your lunch date go?'

'Lousy,' I said.

'Lousy?'

'I don't think Patrick Duffy took to me.'

'You showed him your best side,' my wife said caustically.

'Are you sure you don't know an Yvonne Bloomberg?' I asked.

Later I recalled that decades and decades past I had known an Yvonne. Yvonne Roberts. I don't think any other Yvonne had crossed my path. Yvonne? The name sounded phoney somehow – the assumed name you might find on one of those small cards advertising this or that in a thousand English newsagents' windows:

Massage expertly given by Yvonne. Satisfaction guaranteed. Followed by a phone number.

Yvonne Roberts had not been a bit like that. The opposite would be nearer the truth. After the war, when I was reading English at King's College in the Strand, I had found lodgings in Swiss Cottage. I had met her at one of those unpredictable, lively, bohemian cafés which, at that time, made the district a Mecca for aspiring artists and writers. In those cafés, apart from established refugee authors, one could discover young future novelists like Peter Vansittart, Bernice Rubens, Andrew Salkey. (It was through Andrew that I later went to work for a literary agent – but that is another story.)

Yvonne Roberts was a beautiful 19-year-old girl, the same age as me. Some time in 1948 or 1949 I took her out once to the Everyman cinema in nearby Hampstead to see – I don't know – *Ivan the Terrible* or *The Blue Angel* or was it *The Childhood of Maxim Gorky*? What I can remember with certainty was that Yvonne Roberts, unlike so many of the habitués of those swirling, smoky, talkative cafés, did not have the reputation of sleeping around.

Hans Rosenthal – I can conjure up his leering, forever smiling face now – reckoned Yvonne to be as beautiful as the statue of the Venus de Milo but as cold and frigid as that statue's stone. No doubt he had tried his luck. As for my date with her, I recall how, after our cinema visit – I think it must have been Marlene Dietrich in *The Blue Angel* – I walked Yvonne back down the tree-lined Fitzjohn's Avenue towards her 'digs'. At the gate she smiled with incarnate provocation and, aroused, I moved towards her. She firmly offered me her soft cheek to kiss! 'Goodnight, Peter.'

Some months later she would call in occasionally at one or another of the Swiss Cottage cafés, usually the Cosmo, invariably squired by someone who seemed to be more than twice her age. Was his name Bloomberg? He could well have been one of the many Jewish refugees from Germany and Austria who had settled in the district. For the most part they lived in single, shabby, furnished rooms around and about Swiss Cottage and instigated and supported the cosmopolitan cafés on the Finchley Road where they met, laughed and quarrelled and led their fractured lives. Perhaps Yvonne Roberts had married the fellow to become this Yvonne Bloomberg?

When I myself arrived from Leicester and happened to find 'digs' in Swiss Cottage I was surprised by the visible ubiquity of these refugees who spoke amazingly good English – though, unsurprisingly, with an accent. (The more insensitive bus conductors on the number 13 bus route sometimes used to shout as the bus approached the Swiss Cottage Odeon, 'Next stop – Tel Aviv'. Big joke.)

I soon discovered the Cosmo, the Cordial and the Glass House cafés. Often, of an evening, I would visit one or the other – most commonly the Cosmo because of the pretty girls and the congenial, interesting male company among whom one might encounter not only the youthful novelists but also established refugee writers such as the future Nobel Prize winner, Elias Canetti (I wish I had become his agent) or the poet Erich Fried who was then translating Shakespeare and Dylan Thomas into German.

Theatre people frequented the cafés too: Theodore Bikel who used to play his guitar and sing for us; Lotte Lenya who performed across the road from the Cosmo at the Blue Danube Club and Peter Zadek who later became a famous theatre director in Germany, and who, learning his trade, produced Oscar Wilde's *Salome* at the Rudolf Steiner Hall in St John's

Wood, improbably casting one of the Cosmo writing gang, Bernice Rubens, in the lead.

Some of those Swiss Cottage denizens like Bikel and Lotte Lenya would later head for Hollywood; others had their compasses turned towards jail.

There was Gerald the Hat of whom it was said that he never took off his trilby, not even in the bath. To my mind he never took a bath. Anyway he was fastidious enough when it came to swiping books from Foyles. He would only deign to steal those with pertinent titles: Anthony Hope's *The Prisoner of Zenda*; Dostoevsky's *Crime and Punishment*; Kafka's *The Trial*; Borchert's *The Man Outside*. I remember once seeing Yvonne Roberts carrying away from the Cosmo Arthur Koestler's *Thieves in the Night*. Doubtless she had bought it cheap from Gerald the Hat.

I examined the telephone directory, hoping to discover Yvonne Bloomberg's telephone number. It would be easier to speak to her on the phone than to seek her out at the Belsize Park address she had spelt out. My wife had placed long-stemmed freesias on the small hallstand table and as I searched the directory for the telephone number among the listed Bloombergs of London I became aware of the faint scent of those so feminine flowers.

Yvonne Roberts, I suddenly recalled, always wore perfume in those parsimonious post-war years. She was 'well-groomed'. Once she startled the careless, sartorially austere clientele of the Cosmo by appearing in one of those corduroy 'New Look' suits designed by Christian Dior. Did Gerald the Hat provide her with extra clothing coupons? we all wondered.

Vexed, I discovered that not one of the Bloombergs listed was domiciled at the Belsize Park address. Then I remembered that I could dial 1471 to find out the number. A prose-obsessed woman robot responded: 'You were called today at 11.47 hours. The caller withheld their number.'

I left it at that. I decided if the matter were important enough, and if I hadn't been telephoned by mistake, sooner or later I would receive a repeat phone call from this Yvonne Bloomberg. Weeks passed. I read the new novels and reported on them for the American publisher. I had arranged to see, one day in early October, an ex-client of mine, Tim Howells. He was still with my old firm, Drew and Davidson, but flattered me by seeking my opinion of his work in progress as he used to do in the old days. Tim lived near Reading so I planned to catch a train there from Paddington.

On October 6th, one of those beautiful, elegiac, autumnal days, the sun warm, the air cool, the few clouds in the blue sky moving adagio, I had to postpone my trip to Reading. There had been a fearful calamitous train crash at Ladbroke Grove and no trains were running at Paddington. As I was reading the newspaper account of the accident the telephone rang. At once it occured to me – I do not know why – that the caller would be Yvonne Bloomberg.

I was wrong. It was my daughter who wanted to know if we could look after our grandchildren over the weekend. After I had put the phone down I kept wondering again whether Yvonne Bloomberg would prove to be no other than the once elegant virginal Venus de Milo called Yvonne Roberts. I had now nothing special to do. So, out of curiosity, I decided I would drive over later to the Bloomberg address in Belsize Park.

That afternoon I found myself climbing the stone steps of a crumbling Victorian Gothic house on the borders of Belsize Park and Chalk Farm. In the porch, to the right-hand side of a substantial front door painted a shining funeral black, several cards alerted visitors to the corresponding owners' bells. I pressed the one opposite the starkly printed BLOOMBERG and waited. The window of the ground-floor flat was slightly ajar and I could hear someone ingloriously failing to play 'Three Blind Mice' one-fingered on a piano. Whoever it was – a child? – would start again and fail again to play all the correct notes.

I felt the sun warm on my back as I gave the bell another

press. At last I heard a crackling followed by an indistinct voice. I announced, 'Peter Dawson here.' The door clicked and yielded when I leant against it. I climbed the wide, cinder-coloured, carpeted staircase and Yvonne Bloomberg received me at the open door of her first-floor flat. 'Peter,' she said.

Smiling, she gently touched the sleeve of my jacket and gestured for me to enter through a narrow passage into a disorderly, though capacious, high-ceilinged room. I followed her through the passageway and breathed in an aroma of the perfume she wore. She said to me, as I settled into a far from comfortable chair near a small polished table, 'You haven't changed much. You don't look your age.' She arranged herself opposite me, ensuring that the tall, sky-filled windows with the frayed, heavy, brocaded gold curtains lay behind her so that the sunlight streaming through clung to the outline of her hair like a halo and left her face in shadow.

'And you look like Yvonne Roberts,' I said gallantly.

Actually, even though her face was shaded, I could see how the years had metamorphosised Yvonne Roberts into the image of what might have been her mother. A frail ageing woman now triumphantly inhabited the face and body of the young girl I had once known. This grey-haired ex-Venus de Milo in a correct white blouse and dark skirt seemed to be waiting for me to speak further.

At a loss for words I glanced around the far from elegant drawing room – the best room, I guessed – though absurdly over-furnished with a black leather sofa and huge black armchairs and a particularly ugly, conspicuous sideboard.

'You have a nice place here,' I said.

'This flat's rented,' Yvonne Bloomberg said sharply. 'We've lived here for years and now they want to put the rent up ridiculously. We'll have to move. God knows where. Rents in North London have gone through the roof.' Then, softening her voice, she added, 'Do you remember taking me to the Everyman?'

10

Just then a strange, squawky voice intoned, startling me, 'Speak, you bloody fool.' I turned quickly to see, in the corner behind me, a parrot in a cage. Yvonne Bloomberg laughed. 'Satan rarely utters a word. Only when we have important visitors.'

'Satan?'

But Yvonne returned to her nostalgic theme, 'Yes, you took me to see *Le Jour Se Lève.*

'I thought it was *The Blue Angel.* Marlene Dietrich.'

'No no. They were always showing *The Blue Angel* or *Le Diable au Corps* or *The Childhood of Maxim Gorky* but that night we saw Jean Gabin in *Le Jour Se Lève.*'

She rose smileless. 'I'll put the kettle on. Then I'll give you Dr Simmonds's Journals.'

'Dr Simmonds?'

'He was a wicked man,' she said.

After she had quit the room and I had given a swift glance at the now morosely silent parrot in its cage, I picked up the newspaper that rested on the nearby leather sofa. As I did so I observed a small rip in the shiny dark cover between the cushions revealing its flaxen pale innards.

The newspaper's front page related in detail the horror story of the train crash near Paddington. I had shunned reading all but the headlines that morning but now, in this strange flat, I read the survivors' testimony: the bellowing descriptions of the orange glare from the explosion serving as a background to the scattered silhouettes of passengers in a panic, some careering through the air over pools of fire, and the mobile phones of the dead and the doomed still desperately ringing below the upturned, charred, twisted carriages.

I put the newspaper down for suddenly I had remembered Dr Simmonds. He had resembled someone who could have been a survivor from such a train crash; but I knew that the unhealthy rose-coloured weals on the right side of his cheek were the residual signature of a boyhood Guy Fawkes night accident. He

11

was one of those who used to frequent the Cosmo.

The Cosmo coffee-house annexe, loud with the delirium of youth and saturated with cigarette smoke, where we were wont to congregate, led off from the main, altogether more affluent restaurant. There, Dr Simmonds would occasionally take dinner, presumably after his evening surgery, and later leave the glossy white linen of his table to take his coffee in the annexe.

As an older man, a dozen or so years older than most of us, he was encamped, as it were, beyond the periphery of our circle and he would sit by himself, reading the *Evening Standard* or simply watching the proceedings. I did manage a long conversation with him one rainy night when I happened to sit at his table in the annexe. He confessed that he would have liked to have been a surgeon rather than a GP. 'But that was impossible,' he said, 'after the Guy Fawkes accident when I was a boy.' Then he held up his deformed right hand.

So Dr Simmonds wrote journals. Wicked, Yvonne Bloomberg had said. In what way, I wondered. Pornographic? And why did she want me to read them? Did she know that I had worked for years as a literary agent and thus entertained the half-brained notion that I could sell them for a large sum to a publisher? And how had these journals come into her possession?

Yvonne was taking an incredibly long time to make the tea. I stood up and wandered towards the parrot's cage. I remembered how a parrot had come into a book I had once handled about Byron. As a matter of fact the author was Tim Howells. He had told the story of Byron's lover, Lady Caroline Lamb, who had hopped around the room because her parrot had bitten her big toe. Byron, in a rage, macho, picked up the creature and hurled it across the room. The bird disconcerted him by screaming out, 'Johnny'.

Satan, though, never uttered a word even though I said to it quietly, 'Speak, you bloody fool.' Instead, the parrot lifted one clawed foot, then put it carefully down again and I turned away to the bookcase on the adjacent wall. I read some of the titles:

Hope Against Hope by Nadezhda Mandelstam; *Lost in Translation* by Eva Hoffman; *The Fountain* by Iris Murdoch. Almost all the books were by women.

Hearing voices, I returned to my appointed chair. 'Come in and meet him, Anton.' The man, whoever he was (her husband, Anton Bloomberg?) mumbled something and then I heard footsteps, a far door close, and the thin rattle of china teacups. Yvonne appeared, unaccompanied, pushing a wooden trolley with a plate of small cakes and tea things. I noted four cups and saucers.

Yvonne must have read my thoughts. 'I was hoping Anton and Hugh would join us,' she said. 'But Hugh's in the study with his maps and Anton... well.'

'Maps?'

'Yes, his maps are his dreams.'

I wanted to ask 'Who the hell is Hugh?' Instead I asked, 'Shall I close the door?'

'No, it's all right. Leave it open. An open door is an invitation, isn't it?'

As I began to sip the tea in the delicate cup I heard voices from the rear section of the flat. Raised voices of two men. One began to shout, 'I must go to the funeral. I must, I must.' Yvonne immediately rose and closed the door. Then she went over to a bureau and extracted a blue folder from one of its drawers. She sat down again without passing it over to me.

'I want you to know,' she said, 'that my purpose in life has been and is still to look after Anton. I told him so once in front of Hugh and Hugh said, 'Then your purpose is fulfilled.'

'Anton's your husband?'

'Yes. And now I have to look after both of my two old men, Anton and Hugh. I need money badly, Peter. I want you to sell these journals to a publisher. I think they are very well written.'

'Most people's journals are not publishable,' I said, trying to warn her. 'Nor are they usually meant to be read by others. In a journal or diary the writer is talking to himself. In other forms of prose, even autobiography, the author is speaking to others.'

'Politicians publish their journals and their diaries,' Yvonne said fiercely, 'and they get well paid for it.'

'They are not written as private diary entries. Public figures like politicians know that others will read them. They are offered to publishers as a public secret.'

'If the journals of a politician can interest the public so surely can a doctor's.'

Yvonne turned her head towards the window. The skin on her face was wrinkled but her eyes were uncommonly bright. She was a beautiful old woman.

'You'll read these journals,' she said urgently. 'If I send them off to a publisher I'm told there's not a cat's chance in hell that they'll be fairly assessed. But if they go through such a respected literary agent as you, Peter, then...'

'I'm no longer an agent,' I said. 'I got pushed out years ago. I have very little clout.'

'Please read them,' Yvonne said, passing the blue folder over to me. 'Ten per cent, isn't that right? I mean, that is what an agent takes, isn't it?'

'All right,' I said. 'I'll pass them on to a publisher if I think there's any possibility of them making a book. Otherwise, I fear, I'll just have to return this folder to you. And that's the most likely thing, Yvonne.'

'Thank you,' she said.

Suddenly the door exploded open. A gaunt, ancient man – like someone imagined by Giacometti – stooped, framed in the open doorway.

'Anton!' Yvonne rose from her chair crossly.

'It's too late,' he cried, flinging up his right arm with his thumb also oddly up. 'I told Hugh.'

'Yes, darling,' she said.

'The funeral. It was too late.'

Anton Bloomberg stared at me blankly. 'Too late,' he repeated, addressing me. He turned away and, as he departed down the corridor, I heard him muttering forlornly, 'Too late.'

'He's not been himself for a long time,' Yvonne explained softly. 'You must be puzzled. Anton had an elder sister who, after escaping from Germany, settled in Sweden. In May 1950, she died and Anton was flying from Heathrow for the funeral. The plane was delayed.'

'Fifty years ago?!'

'Lately Anton overheard Hugh and me talking about a Swedish novel called *Dr Glas*. The very words Sweden or Swedish seem to transport Anton back relentlessly half a century. Do you know the dictum of the criminal psychologist Wilhelm Weygandt? "Tell me how you associate and I will tell you who you are." Maybe he was right.'

'I don't follow you.'

Yvonne moved to the door, signalling that my visit was over.

'When you read Robert Simmonds's journals you'll understand much more. And you'll learn, too, why I've waited until now before seeking their publication. It's not just for money, though God knows we need it. Hugh thinks I have a driving inner need to...well...expose myself. Why seek a public confession? he asks.'

She was no longer addressing me. Her eyes, unblinking, stared towards the window. She was speaking to herself. 'It's absurd. I've no need to confess to anyone. I've taken care...'

Yvonne abruptly stopped speaking – as if she had already said too much. I was curious.

'We're all unfathomable. Such irrational creatures, wouldn't you say so, Peter?'

Driving home, the blue folder containing Dr Simmonds's journals next to me on the passenger seat, I thought, why do so many people keep diaries, write journals? Are the majority of them perhaps unsure of their identities and feel themselves to be only partly living, half dead? Convicts in a lenient cosmic prison? Diary-keeping, I suppose, could be a therapeutic exercise, a prescription to prove to its author that he or she is alive. Like the imperative journal pages of a prisoner, the words proclaim, 'I am here, I am alive, I think this, I thought that. This is what I did. This I hope to do.' I suppose, too, that diary-keeping can be so meaningful to some that the author's life could be changed by it. Boswell confessed that he sought out certain adventures so that he could claim them for his diary. On the other hand, keeping a diary can work as a moral force – a confessional mode where the diarist acts as both supplicant and consoling priest.

The traffic was slow-moving as I progressed up Haverstock Hill. And it came to a stop when I was adjacent to Waterstone's bookshop. I had said to Yvonne that a writer is talking to himself only, not addressing others when he makes entries in his journal. But maybe that was not so. Perhaps all diaries and private journals secretly presuppose another reader. When André Gide confessed in his journals to peeing into a chamber pot one night, why did he forcefully add that it was not his usual habit? Gide knew perfectly well what his nocturnal micturating habits happened to be so whom was he addressing? The diarist surely is one who likes to have secrets but hopes that one day his apparently spontaneous effusions, his defenceless unpremeditated scribblings will be whispered to others. No doubt Dr Simmonds must have been one such diarist, I reflected.

The traffic lights changed and, at last, the cars and buses loosened. Ten minutes later I was home.

'Any messages?' I asked my wife.

I settled into my usual armchair. I had certainly stumbled on a weird set-up: an old woman living with two old men and a parrot. Well, two parrots, since one of them kept repeating, 'Too late.' That dictum by Wilhelm Whatsisname about word association – Tell me how you associate and I'll tell you who you are – is the facile sort of thing that would appeal to a Jungian like Patrick Duffy. If this journal is half good enough to be published I wouldn't send it to him. I picked up the blue folder.

PART TWO

December 28th 1949

A CHRISTMAS CARD on the rug near the fender. A winter urban landscape: bare trees, snow on the rooftops, snow on the ground and pointillist snowflakes falling and not falling. It was from my Liverpool cousin, Marjorie. I put the card back on the mantelpiece with the others and stared at the flames in the firegrate. I tried to conjure up the face of my cousin but could not. It's years since I've seen her and the years have crumbled like the grey ash crowning burnt black coal.

Before the war she stayed with us one Christmas. Mother was alive then, of course, and this same living room boasted a Christmas tree and Christmas decorations. It was all indoor greenery, mistletoe, tinsel and tangerines. 'Your mother dotes on you,' Marjorie said accusingly. Well, yes, I was the only person she had.

More and more I dislike this time of the year, this gaping enjambment between Christmas Day and January 1st. The snow, as in Marjorie's Christmas card, is still thinly on the rooftops, brown slush lies in the gutters and the ice covers the Whitestone

Pond. The turkey that my housekeeper, Edith, cooked for me is now completely kaput in the kitchen. The Old Year seems to be yawning in the Waiting Room of Eternity; the New Year somewhere else, limping in with great deliberation, unstoppable. And I shall be forty next March. I can hear your voice, mother – God bless your soul – scolding me, 'Still a bachelor, Robbie dear.'

There have been very few in my Waiting Room today. No one with interesting symptoms. Just the Bewley boy with chilblains, Tom Hobbs with a certificate to sign, Mrs Levy with her recurrent backache. She told me she had chicken for her Jewish Christmas. And, as usual, she offered me a Yiddish apophthegm. 'A chicken these days,' she complained, 'costs gold. You know the Yiddish proverb, doctor? When a rich man is sick he dines on chicken. When a poor man eats chicken, the chicken is sick.'

A quarter of my patients seem to be Jews. Since the war, because of the refugees, Swiss Cottage has become quite a Jewish district. Not as bad as Golders Green, though, where my chess partner, Rhys Morgan, lives. Not that I'm anti-semitic. At least I don't think I am though some of them I do find trying. Pushy. A number of the NW3 Jews who have lived here for generations are, in my view, definitely anti-semitic. They spurn the refugees; don't want to know them. They don't care to reveal to others that they themselves are Jewish – not like Mrs Levy who doesn't care a fig, lets it all hang out.

So many of my Jewish patients suffer from a functional or stress disorder. Perhaps it's all related to their difficult and frightening recent history. They complain of tiredness, precordial pain, indigestion, headaches, amenorrhoea, inability to take a deep breath, fibrositis, insomnia – well I could add to the catalogue endlessly. And all I can do is prescribe a placebo – an iron tonic, a vitamin, or a sedative. Just to reassure them doesn't seem enough.

The ancient Egyptian healers believed, 'He who treats the sick must be expert and learned in the proper incantations and know how to make amulets.' They didn't teach me that when I was a student at the Westminster Hospital Medical School, though some of the prescriptions I wrote out when I qualified in 1934 were hardly more scientifically based. No wonder someone accused doctors of dropping drugs of which they knew little into stomachs of which they knew less. No wonder, too, that people, failed by the medical profession, took cognisance of advertisements for this or that brand of proprietary pill and engaged in self-diagnosis and self-medication.

The phenomenon of proprietary medicines, its success, still obtains even now when these new antibiotics and other medicines have become available. This morning I counted no fewer than thirteen major ads for proprietary medicines in the newspaper that Edith brought in. My eyes roved from ARE YOU WORN OUT WITH CATARRH – *don't delay get Mentholatum Balsam today* JUNO JUNIPAH TABLETS – *You can't even taste them but in no time their gently corrective action means you can taste the joy of feeling and looking your old self again.*

After my late lunch, despite the battleship-grey weather, I walked on the shell of frost that hardened the Heath. There were few others daring the refrigerated air. White steam from their mouths, engine-like, ribboned out and seemed to be pulling them along. On the way back, near the frozen Hampstead pond with its admonitory placard, DANGER, THIN ICE, I was momentarily distracted by a tribe of squawking seagulls circling above my head so that I saw too late Anton Bloomberg, one of my least favourite patients, standing near a nude, desolate tree while his dog, one back paw raised, pissed steam over it. Bloomberg was looking my way. He must have witnessed my fixed loser's smile as I heard his correct, 'Good afternoon, doctor.' I always find his tall, bulky, too physical presence irksome. Irrationally, perhaps. It just irritates me the way he comes too close to me, thrusts his far from pleasant Semite face so close to mine. When I step back a pace he follows me as if magnetised and I feel territorially invaded! Examining patients I must come close to them. Sick patients generally need to be touched; part of their dismay in being unwell is a lack of close human contact for, sometimes, even family members keep their distance, fearing they might catch even a non-infectious illness or simply because unconsciously they fear bad luck. So, perforce, in my consulting room I do allow intimate nearness; but socially I don't wish to breathe in the air they breathe out. Fortunately, now his dog would not permit such intimacy for it pulled at its lead, wishing to get away.

Bloomberg first consulted me just after the war when he learnt with certainty that his wife, whom he had left behind in Hamburg in 1938, had perished in Auschwitz. As a child he had suffered from asthmatic attacks but had grown out of them. Now, knowing his wife was indisputably dead, at night his chest troubled him again. 'In 1938, when I left Germany,' he had told me, 'we had been separated for two years. I didn't know what had happened to her after the November pogrom, the Kristallnacht. We were incompatible. Still, I remember good things, good things.'

I recall suggesting that he should sleep with his head and shoulders raised on four pillows and that he should do breathing exercises. Anyway, recently he has married again – surprisingly, for he is about my age – to that beguiling young girl who used to come into the Cosmo annexe regularly. What she, half his age, saw in him, God knows. Money, perhaps? I understand he has a thriving export-import business. He is one of those enterprising Jews who manage to fall on their feet.

His dog sniffed at me and I wished Bloomberg would control the animal more firmly. The man was too self-absorbed to observe my minor discomfort.

'I've been meaning to consult you, doctor,' he said.

'Your asthma?' I asked.

'No, no. Not so much. I've just been having a lot of indigestion recently.'

'Many people have,' I said as gently as possible. 'Christmas time most of my patients manage to eat too much despite the rationing. Anyway, come to my surgery if your symptoms persist.'

His dog, thank heavens, had ceased its olfactory pursuits. 'It may be something we ate,' Bloomberg agreed. 'My wife hasn't been too well either.'

'I'm sorry to hear that.'

'Oh, she's not too bad. She's gone off this afternoon to see Alec Guinness in *Kind Hearts and Coronets*. Oh no, she's not too bad.'

The dog – of indeterminate breed – was again pulling on its lead, wanting to move on as I did.

'I think your dog hopes to get to the next tree,' I said.

'How do you mean, doctor?'

'Well, I must be getting on too,' I said.

'Yes, yes, of course, this weather. One can't hang about.'

At last I was released. I strolled towards South End Green and reached the final pond, the one on the periphery of the Heath. Again the notice: DANGER, THIN ICE. I heard the sad mewing of inland seagulls and I lingered to watch a duck landing on the iced pond. It extended its yellow, webbed feet forward before coming to a sliding full-stop. How puzzled was it by the solidity of its usual habitat? How much can a duck think? What mental dislocation does it experience when it discovers that the benign waters have magically vanished and some hostile element has replaced them? That fellow, Anton Bloomberg, too, was exiled from his natural home. Awkward. A duck out of water.

Lighting-up time arrives so early. Already the windows of the houses immediately behind the pond blazed their apricot illuminations, their linear reflections smudging the ice. I turned. Bloomberg and his dog were walking nowhere into the dusk along the gravel path, deeper into the eight hundred acres of part grass and part dark woodlands of Hampstead Heath. I remembered how, during the war, a pilot had made a forced landing in a secluded part of it. Lost, he could not believe from his instruments and his maps that he was only some five or six miles from Charing Cross.

Youthful Mrs Bloomberg – now she is a dazzling one to

conjure up in one's mind. She appears so conspicuously different from the sloppy, duffle-coated lot of young people that lounge and laugh in the Cosmo annexe where I sometimes take my coffee. She always reminds me of someone – but I can never place who exactly. Perhaps it's that painting, that self-portrait of Elizabeth Vigée-Lebrun I saw some time ago in the National Gallery: a girl's powdered face, unlined, lacking the signature of experience, beneath a flower-decorated hat with a long, impudent, absurd feather sticking out of it. Perhaps not. Surprising that one with features so refined and sweet should be wedded to one so gross. She is not Jewish; I'm sure she is not Jewish. So. So. He married a shiksa!

When I reached Pond Street and South End Green I decided to visit the Prompt Corner coffee bar. It is the only chess café, as far as I know, in London and the proprietor is a Russian with the predictable name of Boris. It had been a bookshop before the war and George Orwell worked there as an assistant.

I hoped that Rhys Morgan would be around and about so that I could have a game with him. We usually play only on Sundays but Rhys visits the Prompt Corner from time to time. I peered through the lit expanse of plate-glass window. All the chess players, staring at their boards, motionless as if in a dream, were strangers to me so I walked on, homeward, up the slope towards Haverstock Hill and the Town Hall.

It is late. I sit here scribbling because I want to delay going to bed. I do not feel at all sleepy. I keep thinking of how, instinctively, I dislike Anton Bloomberg. Ridiculously, I imagine him, along with his dog, walking on and on across the undulations of Hampstead Heath into the gathering darkness and never coming back.

Certainly, the Heath, after dusk, is no place to loiter on. There are some weird people out there. Not so long ago I heard that someone taking a walk before breakfast saw in the distance, not far from the woods, the configuration of a huge erected crucifix. When he drew close to it he observed a poor bugger nailed to it.

No doubt Anton Bloomberg will buttonhole me sooner rather than later. I see him entering my consulting room – his balding head, the expanse of his resulting forehead, his heavy italic black eyebrows, his hooked nose, his eyes brown and serious as his dog's, his too thick lips opening and closing as he complains about his chest; and coming close to me, so close to me. I see him taking off his shirt as I reach for my stethoscope – his running nose, his wheezing chest, the rust in his pelvis, the Christmas alcohol in his liver, the Scrooge in his soul. I'm not surprised his new wife cleared off to the cinema rather than accompany him on the Heath. They've only been married months and I wouldn't be astounded if already she can't bear his presence.

January 1st
A strange dream last night. I was in the National Gallery staring at that self-portrait of Elizabeth Vigée-Lebrun. No one was about. No guards, no bovine-eyed guards. The Gallery was closed and I, alone, had been allowed privileged entrance. Then the portrait stepped out of the frame. Ridiculous, I know: but she began to undress. I had the impression that she considered her get-up altogether too fancy, that she wanted desperately to change into something demure. A white muslin gown with a sash at the waist suddenly appeared, flung over a nearby chair. As I watched a silent striptease, first one garment discarded, then another (though she kept on her straw hat with its saucy feather) I became aware that Madame Elizabeth Vigée-Lebrun was endowed with a penis, an erect penis. Enraged, I kept yelling at her, 'Get back into the frame.'

Though it's Sunday, Rhys begged off our chess game. On the phone he wished me in a stricken, hangover voice, 'Happy New Year, Robbie,' and then complained that even the bottle of aspirins on the shelf had a headache! 'You're lucky to have missed that party last night,' he said.

I didn't mind being on my own on New Year's Eve. Strange, but I had felt a certain satisfaction that I was sitting down quietly, reading a book, abstemious, virtuous, while others, everywhere, were engaged in corybantic, forced jollity. I retired to bed at eleven o'clock feeling inordinately superior!

This is not the first journal I have begun. When I was twelve or so, my mother encouraged me to keep a record of day to day happenings and to inscribe therein my falsetto thoughts. How she applauded my burgeoning literary efforts. Whatever I wrote in that juvenile journal was for her, I addressed only her and feasted on her approval.

How upset she was when summers later, embarrassed by my boasts and vapourings, I made a small conflagration of that thick exercise book in the firegrate. 'Oh, I wanted to keep that,' Mother said. 'It's part of my life.' And as the paper, charred brown and black, and bits of it, defying gravity, flew up the chimney, I, too, sensed that I was burning up my old self.

Mother has been dead almost ten years. I feel so solitary. Sometimes I put on the wireless, just for company. I have never had a great love, not the kind of love written about in books, in plays, in poetry.

Oh dear, I am becoming maudlin. Welcome 1950.

January 5th

I was very busy this morning. A crowded waiting room and among those glumly sitting there, as if all conversation had been forbidden, I was surprised to see pretty Mrs Bloomberg. No sign of her husband. When I called, 'Next,' a swarthy, thin, scarecrow of a man rose from his chair.

I soon discovered that this patient, a Moslem, suffered from pediculosis. 'What, doctor?' 'Crabs,' I explained. 'Crabs, lice. They have little claws and they've clasped on to your pubic hairs. They feed by plunging their heads into the nest of the hair follicles. That's why you're itching so much. Have you been a naughty boy?'

I prescribed DDT powder – dichloro-diphenyl-trichloroethane – and advised him not to bathe for a few days after applying it. He became agitated, waved his arms, like a wild conductor of an orchestra flaying full blast, allegro. 'I have to bathe each day regularly,' he said. 'It's part of my religion. I have to be clean when I pray.' Cantankerous angels zoomed above my head.

Well, I thought, my mother always used to say when I was a boy, 'Cleanliness is next to godliness.' Maybe. Anyway my Moslem patient had probably slept with someone not too clean. Probably one of those sluts that hang around the disorderly artists in the Swiss Cottage cafés. I waited until he was fully dressed again before remarking, 'Better not to bathe after you've used the DDT powder. Give it a chance to work. Surely you have special dispensations about carrying out your rituals when you're not well?' I had the impression he was about to lose his temper but he merely turned his head, nodded cursorily, and left the consulting room. I wrote up his notes and returned to the waiting room. Mrs Bloomberg had gone.

On my afternoon rounds I parked my new Morris Minor in Buckland Crescent as I needed to give Michael Butler his regular injection of morphine. His growth had been diagnosed too late for radical surgery to be considered. As is customary I have never told him the truth and he, like so many patients similarly afflicted, avoids talking about the prognosis or indeed the real diagnosis. Of course his wife, Rachel, has been informed. And perhaps, in the nadir of night, unable to sleep, Michael Butler confronts his enemy, our enemy, and hears him articulate his real name.

I hear that in the USA some doctors do tell their cancer patients the truth, nothing but the truth, even when they're not pressed to do so. They argue it is unethical to withhold vital facts. I believe, like most British doctors, that such practice destroys hope. It can be a sadistic gesture and lead such patients to turn their faces to the wall. To be sure, these truth-telling doctors are less likely to be sued later by their patients.

Today Michael Butler, despite his terminal cachextic appearance, seemed sinisterly cheerful. I lingered for a while, after the injection, as he reminisced about the Arsenal football team that he used to support and the skill of individual players. 'Hopgood and Male. Terrific backs,' he said, 'And Ted Drake, fearless. This will interest you. There's a doctor playing on the left wing for Arsenal, an Irishman, I think. Amateur, of course. Unusual. I wish I could watch him play.' I nodded, smiled, as if one of these Saturdays indeed that might happen – though I told him no actual lie.

In the living room, which contains full bookshelves on one wall, reaching up almost to the ceiling, Rachel complained, 'He always shows his bright side to you. It's not like that when you've gone. Not like that at all.' I always find it difficult to console Rachel Butler. She is a highly intelligent woman, past middle age. Their children left home long ago. She would have the whole gloomy house to herself in a matter of months. In the hall, which smelt of mice and sweet biscuits, she said, 'Thank you, doctor,' and opened the front door. It was as if she recognised that I can never find adequate, felicitous words for our small, sad dialogues.

January 7th

This afternoon, as soon as it had ceased raining, I visited John Barnes' store in order to use up my clothing coupons. Edith has been nagging me: 'Patients lose their confidence in a poorly dressed doctor.' I believe she imagines that if I don't polish my shoes properly it will signal to all the world that I have little medical expertise. If she had her way, each week day I would be wearing a carnation or some other dulcet flower in my lapel.

At John Barnes I bumped into Mrs Levy whose gaudy toggery competed with the oil pool I had just observed in the street outside the store. She gossiped to me about the refugee Yiddish poet who works as an assistant in the second-hand bookshop in the Swiss Cottage arcade. Before the war he, a Rumanian, was famous among the Jews of Eastern Europe as much for his wild drunken behaviour as for his poetry. The Quakers had managed to extricate him from the clutches of the Gestapo. But his wife had not escaped.

Settled in England the Yiddish poet had written a long book-length elegy for his dead wife. According to Mrs Levy it was reputed to be a masterpiece. Years passed before his wife was discovered in a Displaced Persons' Camp. The poet was summoned to Heathrow to greet her.

'Know what his first words were?' Mrs Levy said, coming to the crux of her story.

'No, what?'

'Listen. He saw her,' she said dramatically, pausing for effect. 'She came towards him smiling. And all he could say was 'You. It's you. You're alive. You have spoilt my elegy.'

I could not help thinking of Bloomberg. Supposing his first wife had also managed to survive the holocaust? What a situation. Maybe his present young wife would not be too disconcerted, relieved even, to discover that she wasn't legally married to the fellow.

Coming out of John Barnes I wished that I had an umbrella. It had started to rain again, a cold damp rain that aspired to become sleet. I had intended to buy an umbrella some time from that shop in the arcade. Why not now? Reaching the arcade I decided first to browse in the second-hand bookshop and take a peek at the notorious Yiddish poet Mrs Levy had told me about.

The musty odour of old books! The possibility of coming

across a neglected esoteric text which, with its secrets disclosed, might change the direction of one's life!

The Yiddish poet, presumably it was he, sat behind a dark-stained desk reading perhaps such a volume. An empty bottle of vodka in front of him made me wonder about his present sobriety. A bell had sounded an old-fashioned tinkle when I entered. He had hardly glanced up. No one else was in the shop. 'Good afternoon,' I said. He did not reply but continued to read his book. I examined his profile. He had, as far as I could see, a bony face and a high forehead beneath reddish grizzled hair.

I turned and pulled out a thick volume from one of the bookshelves. *Leonardo The Florentine*. It had been published by The Richards Press in 1927 and the paper was already tinged yellow. It appeared to be a study in personality. I was tempted to buy it but now that I have ventured on writing a journal I will have little leisure to read such a lengthy volume. I flicked the pages of other books over while the poet, with remarkable insouciance, studied the evidently enthralling pages in front of him. I left without buying a book. The bell sounded again when I opened the door. I don't think he noticed my departure. Next time I go in I'll apologise for disturbing him.

Hearing the announcement of the Saturday football results on the wireless reminded me how, in September 1948, Rhys had persuaded me, for the one and only time in my life, to attend a professional football game. He wanted to watch Cardiff City play Queens Park Rangers. 'Our boys will kick chunks out of them,' I remember Rhys prophesying. 'They're a lot of sopranos, I'm telling you.' It turned out to be a 0-0 acrimonious draw.

I found the game boring. I enjoyed for a change though, the exhilaration of belonging to a crowd, shouting in unison – the comradeship. The Nazis must have felt that way, losing momentarily their individual identity, losing their private burdens as they held high their swastika banners and torch-marched through the night towards their floodlit, fulminating, hypnotic Führer.

Had I been born in Germany, would I, like so many, have welcomed the irresponsibility of conformity and its ease – freed from the pressures of choice? Rhys reckons I have a vestigial sprinkling of Nazism in my soul and that I would have responded to the bugle-call of Wotan. He even suggests I'm a bit anti-semitic and blunder into saying things Jews might find upsetting. I don't think so. As I've said to him, if I was so transparently anti-semitic why should so many of the Chosen Race choose me as their doctor?

I don't believe I would join any bloody-toothed pack. My dislike, say, of Anton Bloomberg may be irrational but it's not because he's a Jew. It is because he's Anton Bloomberg. Besides, when it comes to patients I find offensive, conscious of my private feelings, I compensate by being particularly scrupulous and caring, be they Jew or Gentile.

January 8th
Rhys Morgan arrived late for our Sunday afternoon chess game. He had lunched at the Blue Danube Club (whale steak) and had fallen in with congenial company.

'The Middletons were there again,' he told me. 'That Amy, she's something, you know, a celestial sinfonietta with the accent on sin.'

As we arranged the chess pieces Rhys continued to focus on the physical attributes of Frank Middleton's wife. 'She's odiously beautiful,' he sighed. 'Ugly as Ugolino but has a voluptuous figure like Jane Russell's.'

Rhys, who like me is a bachelor, amuses me when he speaks about women. His liaisons have never lasted. Ever since I've known him, since 1942, he has habitually likened his three-night-stand partners to enshrined film stars such as Jane Russell. His most recent 'ex' had been 'a dead ringer for Joan Fontaine'.

Before we commenced our chess joust Rhys remarked,

'Anyhow, Amy asked me about you, what sort of a doctor you were. I let on you give a minto away with every prescription.' I hardly know the Middletons. Rhys introduced me to them just before Christmas when I went to the Blue Danube with him to hear Lotte Lenya sing.

'Frank Middleton's got a very hush-hush job with the Air Ministry. I don't know what. He visits Germany a lot,' said Rhys thoughtfully. 'Anyhow he smells of marmite.'

'Come on,' I said. 'White moves first, remember?'

We generally talk very little during our games of chess. Rhys sometimes says out loud, addressing himself, 'Wait a minute,' or expostulates, 'Not too bad, not too good,' but this afternoon, soon after he had moved his pawn to Q4, he leant back in his chair so that it balanced precariously on its two wooden legs and talked between moves.

'From one or two confiding hints from delectable Amy I gather Frank's washing some of those Nazi scientists with very British Persil. Gettin' those rocket buggers to sign up on our side. We need 'em to hot up the Cold War. As for Amy – there's limitless enchantment there, boy.'

'You're smitten by the lady.'

'No, no. She's married anyhow. She's Paradise Lost.'

During the first year of the war Rhys had served in the RAF. 'I was just a scruffy erk,' he had told me. After a few months he had been invalided out – he would never say why. In civvy street, when the bombing of London became the Blitz and property prices plunged, Rhys had bought a large, many-windowed house in West Heath Drive for a song and had let off rooms. He still does. When asked, 'Occupation?' he replies, 'Gentleman.'

Rhys's dark head bent over the board and I thought of his gift of drawing strangers' secrets out of them quickly. (He would soon know more about Frank Middleton's daunting intimacies.) The first day I met Rhys he enquired without a trace of embarrassment how my right hand had become deformed and my 'right cheek disfigured so interestingly'. In no time at all I

32

had found myself relating the story of my childhood firework accident to this Welsh stranger – the irresponsibility of my careless father who, soon after, took off with his mistress to Canada, leaving my mother bereft.

Rhys looked up, caught my stare, smiled companionably, and said, 'Not too good, not too bad,' before moving his castle to prevent my knight from forking him.

After driving Rhys back to his Golders Green home I manoeuvred the car into the garage. From the frosty garden path I gazed up beyond the rooftops of the house opposite at the obvious full moon, and higher still towards the conundrum of infinity, the suspended stars – those outposts of theology. I'm not religious. Since my mother died I no longer go to church or pray. But the night sky with its moon and all its stars prompts a man, does it not, to contemplate the beginnings of the universe, the worlds beyond, and the birthplace of Time. Who made God, Mother?

I can sympathise with that Welsh divine whom Rhys once told me about. One morning, on horseback, he rounded a green corner of Wales to find before him a spectacular vista which stretched on and on, meadow after meadow, to a glinting river and then further still to the grandeur of the rising mountains. Overcome, tears in his eyes, the priest dismounted, fell on his knees and cried, 'Well done, God.'

Before I reached the porch I heard the far drone of an invisible aeroplane on its night-sky journey. Its noise increased, it throbbed threateningly, and I thought of the war, of the bombing of London, of the Ack-Ack guns' cacophony from Primrose Hill and of those nights when I watched my own shadow lengthen, become a giant's, as I hurried away from prodigious fires to find a location, a sanctuary, where I could stitch up the skin wounds of those who had been lanced by malevolent flying glass.

I remembered how once, the searchlights fumbling the sky, the guns and planes too raucous, the explosions too near, I ran home and almost stumbled into a large bomb crater with a smell of fresh cinders. I heard so clearly shrapnel clanging repeatedly against the lids of nearby metallic rubbish bins. Those nights of fire and screams, I sensed, like Peer Gynt, that nothing truly dreadful would happen to me. It was easy to appear brave. It was as if that long ago night of the fireworks accident had given me immunity against more lethal conflagrations.

Indoors now, in this creaking house, like a child I feel wary, if not a little afraid. But of what? I wish I had someone dear beside me, someone who would touch my shoulder reassuringly and announce with indisputable certainty that all is well, and that all manner of things will continue to be well.

January 9th

I cut myself shaving this morning. I kept staring at my own face with enmity until it began to stare back at me. Let me be frank. I forget most of the time about the ridged, raw-coloured fire-stain on my right cheek. If it were not for that conspicuous blemish I think I would be almost good-looking. As it is, my visage to others must be displeasing. Yet if I turn my head to the left, I observe in the mirror Mr Hyde vanishing, replaced magically by Dr Jekyll.

Am I ineluctably vain? Women who are conscious of their posture and appearance make a point of sitting in a certain way and where the light is not cruel to them. And haven't I, on self-conscious occasions, settled myself in a chair so that Mr Hyde is hidden from the one opposite me? If I commissioned someone to paint my portrait, I would, like the Duke of Urbino who had one eye gouged out in battle, insist on showing my Piero my agreeable profile.

I wonder if some shaded verity resides in the primitive notion that the soul of a person is reflected in his countenance, that if a man or a woman is born ugly or becomes ugly it is a sequel to a personal or familial disorder. As a small boy, before that horrendous Guy Fawkes night, I was convinced of it. When our maid took me to my first Cowboy film I was utterly confused. For when I asked her, 'Who's the good man, who's the baddy?' her answer made me want to cry. I had judged the villain to be infinitely more handsome than the hero sheriff.

The child in me, I think, wants beautiful Mrs Bloomberg to be good; the ugly Mr Bloomberg to be bad.

And what of myself? Don't my two profiles represent the duality in my nature? Isn't the fire-scar on my cheek the reflection of the fire-scar in my soul? The faces of the wretched and the unhealthy are rarely pleasant to look upon. Health flatters us as cleverly as skilful make-up. Don't we say, 'You look well,' with English understatement or, more directly, 'You look good.'

Leering at the bathroom mirror this morning I saw Dorian Gray in his dilapidation.

January 12th

Last night Charlie Forster, friend of my medical student days, invited me to have dinner with him at Kettner's in Soho. He was in debt again. This time not so much through gambling. He had borrowed money from the bank to join a group of risky doctors who, having contracted out of the National Health Service, had put up their plate in Harley Street. The sums advanced to Charlie had proved insufficient.

To my mind some of the people he associates with need to scrub their hands strenuously to keep their fingernails clean. Tony Dickinson, for instance, who, when I qualified, had been house physician to that eccentric Westminster Hospital neurologist, Hildred Carlill. Dickinson, like his boss, would hypnotise his patients. 'Repeat after me. I must not have intercourse with my wife while she's in the later stages of pregnancy. Once again, repeat, I must not have intercourse with my wife...'; also that oleaginous poker-playing osteopath friend of Charlie's, Tom Taylor, who confided to me that his patients consisted of 'debutantes and high-class prostitutes, some of whom are indistinguishable from each other.'

'When I've got some melon in the pantry, Robbie, I'll let you have the money back pronto,' Charlie said.

'You should have joined the NHS,' I scolded him.

'They don't pay enough,' said Charlie contemptuously. 'Those BMA Council members sold out too cheaply to Nye Bevan and that gang. You're not going to vote for that mouse Attlee, are you Robbie, in next month's election?'

The British Medical Association had negotiated the new National Health salaries for doctors based on what they had previously earned in private practice. But many GPs had fiddled their income tax returns for years so, now, in the NHS, doctors found themselves somewhat financially disadvantaged.

Our meal over, when we were being served coffee, Charlie, to my surprise, extracted two pre-war looking, rare cigars from the inside pocket of his jacket. He smelt one and passed me the other.

I could not refuse Charlie the money – quite a sum – he needed. During our first clinical months at Westminster Hospital, when we were both on the same surgical 'firm' and had 'walked the wards' together, I had found it difficult to cope. It had been the consequence of a combination of things – or to use medical jargon, my confusion of mind had a multifactorial aetiology.

My mother had just died and I missed her so. (I still do.) In addition, there was the initial trauma of having to deal for the first time with suffering patients and so many things were for the first time: the first time to take blood from a vein, first lumbar puncture, first time to assist at a major operation, first post mortem, first death of a patient I had attended in the ward.

I had become depressed, unable to sort out mother's legacies. My grandfather's South African gold-mining shares had to be sold in order for me to continue my studies at Medical School. According to Charlie, he had discovered me staring in a trance-like state at the khaki-coloured waters of the Thames as if I had been treated by Hildred Carlill himself.

In my despondency I became increasingly dependent on Charlie Forster. He had efficiently discussed elusive matters with the lawyers and dealt with the stockbrokers. In short, on the whole, he had been generously supportive.

Besides, our acquaintanceship goes back a long time, even before we joined the same surgical year in our fourth year of study. Earlier, during our Anatomy course in the Dissecting Room, we were assigned the same, helpless, naked cadaver. I remember how initially Charlie could not bear to contemplate the features of the corpse. Each session, before picking up his silver-coloured scalpel, he would ceremoniously place a cloth over the face before dissecting his half of the body. I think he would have been happy to have given the dead man an anaesthetic. His fastidiousness did not endure. After a few weeks, one day he dropped his lit cigarette accidentally into the open cavity of the dead man's abdomen and, unthinkingly, he picked up the cigarette, put it back in his mouth, and went on dissecting with no sense of disquiet or disgust.

We used to study our medical textbooks together – testing each other's memory as we did so. Charlie, in many ways, had been a typical athletic, poker-playing medical student. He married a nurse before he even qualified and I saw less and less of him. When we did meet I found him much more cynical, much more interested in money. 'There are only two kinds of patients, Robbie. The rich and the poor.' And I learnt from other contemporaries at Westminster how he had begun to spend innumerable hours at horse-racing events and at the greyhound tracks. I was not surprised to hear that he had opted out of the National Health Service.

'Where did you get the cigars from, Charlie?' I asked.

He winked. When we left Kettner's we strolled through the neon-lit sleaze of Soho with girls standing in doorways, muttering as we passed, 'Want a virgin, honey?' At Leicester Square we parted ways so that I could catch a Northern Line Tube home and for Charlie to hail a taxi.

That loan? Am I a mug?

January 14th

I can't help thinking about my loan to Charlie. Will I ever get it back? Such a pity when you lose the true friendship of your youthful days. I would never have guessed how Charlie would change. Change utterly. I remember how his eyes used to brighten when he spoke about one of his heroes, Philippe Pinel, consultant physician to Napoleon and medical superintendent of the Bicêtre hospital in Paris during the late 18th century. Unlike his contemporaries Pinel reacted sensitively to the mentally sick. The treatment of those poor wretches at that time consisted of bloodlettings, vomits and purges. They were banished (unless they happened to be rich) to Auschwitz-like institutions, stripped naked, chained, and led to a dark cell or dungeon. I recall how Charlie related with such innocent delight how Pinel unchained an English Captain who had been manacled for forty years. 'His cell door was left open,' Charlie said, 'and with tottering steps the Captain walked outside, gazed up at the sky in pure wonder, exclaiming, "How beautiful, how beautiful," before returning to the cell of his own accord.'

In our student days Charlie was as idealistic about Medicine as I was. I like to think I still am. But only the past is unchangeable.

The phone after 10.30 p.m. I thought, 'Damn it all, a night call. Where? Who?' It was an emergency according to Mrs Levy but fortunately not a medical one.

'I suggested you, doctor, a scientific person.'

'What?'

'One of the panel of our Charity Brains Trust has dropped out, so I suggested you, excuse me. And the committee said wonderful, if you'd agree. Sunday afternoon at the Broadhurst Gardens Centre – you know, near John Barnes, behind the Finchley Road Tube station.'

I explained to her that I had other commitments on Sunday afternoons – I was not anxious to miss my chess game with Rhys. I prevaricated.

'Listen,' she said, 'you'd not be substituting for a nobody. You'll be substituting for Professor Joad. Mrs Bloomberg said you'd be a splendid substitute.'

'Mrs Bloomberg? Is she on your committee?'

'Please,' Mrs Levy continued, 'without somebody clever like you we'll be in Shloch Street.'

'Shloch Street?'

'It's charity. Charity. Agree, doctor, please. Charitable acts, excuse me, that require self-sacrifice will be remembered by God in the hour of the world's calamity.'

'Who else is on the panel?' I asked.

'Well,' Mrs Levy answered. 'We have to compete with all the political meetings going on because of the election coming up. So we couldn't ask our local MP, er Henry Brooke, or Maurice Edelman – the best-looking MP, don't you think? So there's Cecil Forbes, the author of *The Battle of Balaclava*, Jane Fox, our mighty scholar of a secretary, my husband, and you substituting for Professor Joad. We'll have plenty of people coming because Professor Joad's name is on the poster.'

Mr Levy? He hardly ever spoke. Shorter even than his wife, he resembled a five-foot corpulent baby wearing glasses. He always lets Mrs Levy do the talking. If silence were golden then this bespectacled homunculus could sit comfortably on the throne of King Midas.

I agreed to join the panel finally. I was curious to see how Mr Levy would fare. Besides, Mrs Bloomberg was likely to be in the audience.

January 20th

The local newspaper, much to my astonishment, reported what I had said at the Broadhurst Gardens Brains Trust:

In response to a question about Euthanasia, Dr Simmonds argued, 'Too many patients at the portals of death are kept alive needlessly because the physician cannot face the religious and

*ethical problems he would have to confront.' He went on to say,
'In our hospitals and in general practice the medical imperative
is to foster health, to make people well again. But comes the hour
when physician and surgeon are helpless. We may put an animal
out of its misery but the law and the doctor's own training often
inhibit him from being truly human at the last.'*

*Mrs Jane Fox of Belsize Park Square, told the sparse
audience that Pliny had, in his day, complained that physicians
were the only citizens who could kill others with sovereign
impunity and Mr Levy interjected with a Yiddish proverb – 'If the
rich could hire others to die for them what a wonderful living the
poor could make.'*

The report was more or less accurate. I had argued that in
medicine there was a time to kindle and a time to quench. Mr
Levy had not spoken all the evening except to come forth with
that reported Yiddish proverb. I fear they raised very little money
for their charity. Only a couple of dozen people attended the
Brains Trust, among them Yvonne Bloomberg, who, I observed,
arrived unescorted.

Each time I was called upon to speak, or when I intervened, I
fancied that she listened to me with admiring intensity and,
indeed, made notes, which I found very flattering. Afterwards
she told me that she kept a diary – hence the note-keeping. I
confessed that I did too. A sporadic journal, 'where I address my
future self'. I hope I didn't sound too pompous.

'There's a novel which I think would interest you then,' she
said. 'A Swedish novel. It's about a doctor. He also keeps a
journal. I must lend it to you.'

I was tempted to ask her why she had appeared briefly in the
waiting room of my Surgery. And why she had not yet returned.
I didn't though. I feared such questions might be too intrusive. I
think she will come in her own good time. While we conversed
I became self-conscious, aware that she could examine closely
my blemished features. She, herself, has such a vulnerable
beauty and such a fetching smile it makes me breathless.

Euthanasia. Absurd that I keep recalling not the deaths of patients but the expiring of one particular cat. It happened years ago when I was a sixth-form schoolboy. Black Chin, more a kitten than a fully-grown cat, had been caught unawares by a dog so that one of its back legs was badly broken. Across the road, in the house that Mr Bailey and his family now occupy, lived a retired vet, old Mr Edwards. So I took Black Chin, cradled in my arms, over to our neighbour. It was summer, I remember, and the street smelt of tar.

Mr Edwards gave one quick glance at our cat before leaving the room. 'Just a minute,' he said. He had departed, I assumed, to fetch some animal medicament or perhaps to wash his hands.

Old Edwards, at the best of times, had a slovenly appearance, but that afternoon he had opened the front door to me, grossly unshaven, with one eye half-closed because of the smoke from a cigarette swirling up from his mouth. He wore no jacket, his shirt was collarless and his braces held up trousers much too large for him.

He returned to the room carrying a huge syringe and sermon-faced, commanded me to hold Black Chin tight. Imperturbably, he picked up the cigarette that he had left smouldering in the ashtray, took a quick puff at it, replaced the 'dibby' in the ashtray, before plunging the needle into the thigh of Black Chin. What I witnessed then was extraordinary. I shall never forget it. The young cat jumped with unnatural kinetic strength out of my arms and leapt almost to the ceiling. I do not exaggerate – it hurled itself upwards that high above my head. Despite having only three available legs it gave four or five looping hops around the room, mad with energy, before falling down dead.

'Strychnine,' explained Mr Edwards, picking up the cigarette again.

After the Brains Trust meeting, while we were having coffee and biscuits, Mrs Levy asked me whether I thought she should consult an osteopath about her arthritic back. Tom Taylor came into my mind. He had told Charlie Forster and me how he used a range of electrical appliances in treating his society patients. Fingering his bow-tie he had opined, 'Suggestion is a powerful therapeutic ally. A sharp tickle and prickle from an electric current can work wonders for an Eskimo Nell as it can for Lady Gullible's poor aching back.' I did not refer Mrs Levy to his care. I'm not that anti-semitic.

On arriving home I recalled Mark Twain's pithy remark, 'To ask a doctor's opinion about osteopathy is like consulting Satan for information about Christianity.' I should have quoted that to Mrs Levy. Too late.

January 24th
Edith, my housekeeper (she comes in from Hendon five days a week) has asked me to consider putting central heating into the house, as is the custom in America. I'm not convinced it's healthy to do so. I remember that at one time the *British Medical Journal* printed a survey about factory workers – how those who toiled in an environment kept cool and with a high humidity caught head colds much less frequently than workers in other, warmer sections of the factory.

I'm certainly one for keeping the bedroom window open at night. Being single I can do as I wish. I don't draw the curtains either. I like the street lamplight to filter through. I like to see, when I'm still awake at night, supine in bed, the swift, shimmering headlight reflections of the desultory late traffic racing across the ceiling.

I can do what pleases me. How does that line go? – I am the master of my fate. I don't have to argue with a pettifogging, obdurate wife about leaving the windows open on drastic January nights or whether the curtains should be fully drawn. And a hot-water bottle in a man's bed can surely offer him as much radiated comforting warmth as the 98.4 Fahrenheit degree heat of a woman's proximate body. It's more of a sedative too! Do I miss out on sex? Masturbation has its advantages. As Rhys once joked, 'That way you meet a better class of person.'

When Rhys made that jocund remark, I thought how vulgar. Now I surprise myself and castigate myself for frivolously bothering to repeat it here.

It's late. Stochastic thoughts. It has suddenly struck me: could that schoolgirl whom I encountered in the Glass House Café at Swiss Cottage in 1946 be none other than Yvonne Bloomberg?

After the annual reunion dinner of the Westminster Hospital Old Students, I had managed to catch the last bus back to Swiss Cottage. Hours had passed since our meal and I felt peckish again. When I alighted at the bus stop opposite the dark Swiss Cottage Odeon I fancied I could eat something-on-toast. All the shops were closed, the Cosmo too; but I could see ahead the Glass House still wonderfully lit up – the only place open. Otherwise this stretch of the Finchley Road looked desolate. The row of ruined, once elegant, three-storey houses on the other side of the street showed no friendly lights. No one lived in them. They were ghost houses. Having been gutted during the war by incendiary bombs only their handsome façades remained untouched, resembling opera scenery.

In the Glass House I sat on one of the red-leathered high stools which surrounded the horseshoe-shaped bar. I hardly noticed the schoolgirl sitting opposite me. I do recollect that for a brief moment I considered a girl of such an age should not be out and about at this long past midnight hour. Absorbed in eating my Welsh rarebit and half listening to the conversation of two men, one somewhat drunk, sitting my side of the bar, I did not observe the girl quit the café.

After I had paid my bill I discovered her loitering outside on the dark pavement. Immediately she appealed, 'Sir, please could you

43

see me home? I'm frightened to go down the side-streets on my own.' It was a moonless night and though the war had been over for more than a year most of the lampposts were useless, their bulbs missing or broken. Except for the incandescent glare from the Glass House behind me it could still have been the Black Out.

'I live in Netherhall Gardens,' said the girl.

It would have been churlish of me to have refused. To accompany her home entailed only a minor detour on my part. We walked together along the somnolent Finchley Road. Opposite John Barnes the schoolgirl halted, surveyed the sky, and said, dramatically, as if rehearsed, 'Behind the clouds the stars shiver. Like me they're frightened of the evil in the world.' When we resumed walking she chattered on in this other-worldly manner. I sensed this schoolgirl was trying to impress me. Or perhaps she had seen too many of those poetry-dramas by T.S.Eliot, Christopher Fry and Ronald Duncan which the Mercury Theatre staged at Notting Hill Gate.

As we climbed the alleyway that led off from the Finchley Road towards Netherhall Gardens she said, 'On the Second Day of Creation my RI teacher says God brought forth the firmament, hell, fire and the angels. Do you believe that?' I could not help smiling indulgently, 'No, I don't,' I said.

She remained pensively quiet until we had threaded through to the other end of the alleyway into the broader street. 'You don't believe in angels,' she said, in a tone that suggested that as a result I was a person of little consequence and that I had disappointed her. Before I could answer she grabbed my arm frantically as if endangered and, simultaneously, I heard footsteps the other side of the road. They suddenly ceased. I strained to peer across to the opposite pavement but could see nobody at all. 'I'm afraid,' the girl whispered. I lost my superior complacency when she, inordinately terrified, came so close to me I could feel her trembling.

'Don't move, please, don't say anything,' she said, almost inaudibly.

Somebody was standing immobile across the road. Why? I felt threatened, indeed annoyed, and I called out, 'What do you want?' Whoever it was did not reply but the sound of his footsteps resumed and gradually diminished.

The girl unfastened herself from me. 'Please,' she said, 'don't ask me any questions. Don't ask me who that shadow was.'

I was now adrenally awake. I wanted to dump this odd, somewhat crazy schoolgirl as soon as possible and make for the ordinary security of my home. I continued to sense imminent danger as we progressed up the incline past the lightless houses of the deserted street. I was relieved when we rounded the corner and could see, in Netherhall Gardens itself, up the hill, nearer to Fitzjohn's Avenue, a nightwatchman warming himself beside a brazier of glowing red coal. Close to his hut, a looming, massive shape of a steamroller was just visible.

'They're mending the road,' I said inanely.

When we passed the watchman I greeted him and we walked about another thirty yards before the girl pointed to a pitch-dark large house. 'This is where I live,' she said. No welcoming light shone behind the glass of the front door for this truant schoolgirl. For Christ's sake, it was one o'clock in the morning. Her parents should surely have at least left a light on in the hall.

'Don't your parents wait up for you?' I asked.

To my astonishment she grabbed my wrist and tried to pull me into the bosky, dark, front garden.

'Come,' she said.

There was no mistaking her erotic intent.

'No,' I said, disengaging myself with no little difficulty.

Again she tried to draw me close. 'Sorry,' I muttered and she, wordless, broke away and rushed through the gate up the path to the dim porch steps.

Once she was in the porch I could no longer see her. I hoped she had not been locked out. I waited until I heard her turn the key in the front door. I was free at last, shot of the girl, responsible only for myself. I walked swiftly up to Fitzjohn's

Avenue and beyond, homeward, through the hushed, panther-dark streets of Hampstead.

Ridiculously, she had asked me, 'Do you believe in angels?'

And despite her explicit yearning for sexual contact there seemed something angelically innocent about her. Her schoolgirl comments – the stars being frightened – that sort of thing – her attempts at being poetic.

Those footsteps I heard that ceased and then resumed on the other side of the road puzzled me most. To whom did they belong? Someone she knew waiting for her to arrive home? Her trepidation surely had not been simulated? She had palpably quivered. She had grabbed me in a panic and I had felt her shaking with seemingly pure fear.

Another enigma: why was such a young girl permitted to be out so late? The substantial house she lived in suggested she had affluent parents; but what kind of people were they who did not bother to wait up for a schoolgirl daughter out on a post-midnight caper?

The next morning, after my surgery, I retraced my steps to Netherhall Gardens. I don't know why I hoped that the girl would come out of the house just as I happened to pass by. Curiosity, I suppose. Or subliminal inklings of what, on arriving, I would discover?

The steamroller, with men carrying busy shovels either side of it, worked the tarred macadam of the road. I paused by the watchman's hut, amazed. The schoolgirl's house was curtainless, empty. A FOR SALE estate agent's board was in conspicuous evidence the other side of the overgrown hedge. The dishevelled wilderness of the front garden indicated that the house had been uninhabited for months, if not years. I cannot exaggerate the degree of my bewilderment. That girl had surely gone into that abandoned house. Incontrovertibly, I had heard the key turn in the lock. It had been very dark but how could I not have apprehended that this massive house was empty? How could I have missed the FOR SALE sign?

46

Several nights following that puzzling incident I visited the Glass House for a coffee. Would I have recognised her if she had returned to the café's horseshoe bar? I had merely glanced at her when she sat opposite me. Afterwards, outside, I had only seen her as if behind a glass darkly. No one resembling her turned up.

Four years have passed and now, at this midnight hour of January 24th, I wonder whether that spurned oestrogen-loaded schoolgirl could have been the younger self of angelic Yvonne Bloomberg? No, no. It cannot be. Their ages would not match – unless that schoolgirl was by some years older than I had estimated.

January 26th

This afternoon, after I had given Michael Butler his necessary morphia injection, his wife tackled me again in the hallway. 'I read the report in the *Hampstead and Highgate Express*,' she said. 'So you favour euthanasia, doctor?'

'Well,' I said, 'not exactly. I mean it's illegal, Mrs Butler.'

'But you would...'

'At present,' I interrupted her, 'we must only think of mobilising Michael's will to live. He is not yet defeated.'

'But when the time comes?'

'He is not alone,' I said. 'Pain does isolate people but you are with him. You, I'm sure, reveal your love to him every day.'

'Fat lot of good that does.'

I hesitated. 'You're wrong,' I said.

'When it's time for Michael to go,' she almost whispered, 'you will, won't you, doctor?'

At Michael Butler's house I had spoken about the will to live. I have had patients who have turned their faces to the wall and have quickly deteriorated. Others have survived for many more months than predicted because they refused mentally to surrender to their invincible diseases. If some doubt the power of the mind over soma they need to consider the magic of omens and portents and those incantations which lead to voodoo deaths.

I sometimes think that some patients unconsciously choose cancer as an alternative to going mad. Perhaps Michael Butler is one such. Before his illness, following the death of his father, he had been almost psychotically depressed. Now, despite all the pain he experiences I have the impression that he is much more mentally balanced.

When I, myself, became ill after the loss of my mother I, a medical student, had despaired to such an extent that I considered walking into the Thames. I felt such an indescribable sense of separation from others. I belonged to no one. They made me consult the hospital psychiatrist who, insensitively, bluntly, suggested that I loved my mother too much and that with her passing I should become attached to another person. So easy to say! He quoted Freud: 'In the last analysis we must love in order not to fall ill and must fall ill when we cannot love.' Perhaps. Anyway I recovered and, fortunately, have not contracted a physical illness in exchange for my mental depression.

January 27th
What a strange thing it is to keep a journal? It is a way of living one's life twice.

The post was later and larger than usual. A number of letters had been forwarded on to me by the local newspaper. My contribution to the Brains Trust forum had stirred some to argue that there was such a circumstance as ethical murder – that it should be lawful to bring about a painless death for long-suffering patients. Others, outraged, abused me. One correspondent wrote at length – six pages of microscopic handwriting – about the evil in the world and why our omnipotent, intrinsically beneficent Creator permitted it. I think he favoured the religion of Zoroaster and believed that I was a disciple of Ahriman, the principle of evil. This odd letter was unsigned.

A parcel arrived also, a slim novel entitled *Doctor Glas*. When I opened the book's cover a note dropped out. 'My dear Dr Simmonds, I enclose the novel I rambled on about the other evening. Please accept it as a gift from me. Because it purports to be the journal of a doctor I think it may interest you. It was a delight to hear you speak at Broadhurst Gardens. I've put down in my diary one of your remarks – "More saints seek to become doctors than doctors would become saints." I hope our paths cross again soon. With esteem, Yvonne Bloomberg.'

The novel turned out to be by a Swedish author, Hjalmar Söderberg. It had been published in 1905 and had become valued as a contemporary classic. I read the blurb on the dust-cover: 'The haunting tale of Dr Glas takes place during the closing years of the nineteenth century and concerns the elderly Rev. Gregorius and his pretty young wife who has taken a lover. Dr Glas resolves to help Mrs Gregorius with whom he has become emotionally involved. The uxorious pastor dies of poison. The outcome of his death and Dr Glas's unforeseen reactions to it, bring the story to a close...'

The publisher went on to quote William Sansom – curiously enough, one of our Swiss Cottage writers who can be seen occasionally in the Cosmo and habitually in the Swiss Cottage pub. Sansom wrote, 'When the book first came to me I got that marvellous rare feeling, after the first page or two, of being quite certain I was in the hands of a master... That this is a work of art and a masterpiece is to my mind, unassailable.'

I sat at my desk for a long time. Was this gift from Yvonne Bloomberg some sort of coded message, a cry for help? Did she imagine that I could help her to be released from her older, offensive husband? I reread the blurb which indicated that Dr Glas had violated the ethics of his profession and used 'a highly unorthodox method of helping her...' I wanted to laugh. I don't know why. I just wanted to laugh.

Though patients were accumulating in the waiting room for my morning surgery I began to read the novel. On the third page Dr Glas muses, 'Mrs Gregorius, yes! That was a queer visit she paid me the other day. She came to my surgery hour. I noticed clearly when she arrived, but although she had come in good time she let others who had come after her see me first. At last she came in. Blushed and stammered. Finally blurted out something about having a sore throat. Well, it was better now – I'll come back tomorrow, she said. Just now I'm in a hurry... so far she hasn't come back.'

I put down the novel. What game is this? Why has Yvonne Bloomberg given me this particular book? Is it just because I'm a doctor who keeps a journal or has she a more arcane motive? Maybe she's desperate. Mrs Bloomberg appeared at my surgery and then vanished before I could call her in. So far, like Mrs Gregorius, she has not come back. Is she, in some pernicious way, under the influence of this novel?

It was time to open the door to the waiting room. Even before I did so I guessed that I would find Anton Bloomberg there.

I returned to sit behind my desk. Bloomberg brought the patient's chair obliquely forward, as far as he could, as if trying to make contact with me. He spoke softly, haltingly, conspiratorially. 'My wife, Yvonne... I've tried to persuade her to come and see you... I don't know, maybe she ought to be referred to a gynaecologist. Well, to be frank, doctor, I, er, well we've been married now three months and er... she's not still a virgin, not quite... Her welfare is very important to me but... right? Everything else... '

His wife, I eventually was able to elucidate, experienced vaginismus each time he attempted to penetrate her. '... Ever since the first night,' he said, 'it's been hopeless.'

I had a disgusting vision of this tall gross man naked and gorged, trying to force himself on his gentle young wife. I expressed my sympathy for him, of course, and suggested that he should be patient and court her tenderly. 'I've seen cases like this before,' I reassured him. 'Leave her unmolested for a month. You say you have twin beds in the bedroom. For a while you should consider separate bedrooms. It would be easier for you, too.'

'Molested?' he said, annoyed. 'Do you know she hit me the first night?'

'Molested is not the right word. But you know what I mean.'

'She complains I raped her on our honeymoon. What can I do? She's never been touched by a man nor has she touched a man. It's 1950 not 1850.'

'You must take it slowly,' I reiterated. 'It'll turn out all right in the end.'

How glib and insincere doctors have to be sometimes. And how tiresomely necessary it is to tell benign lies. Before he left my consulting room I asked Bloomberg about his chest.

'I wheeze a bit at night,' he admitted, 'especially in this cold weather, but nothing much. And we have central heating in our flat, you know, which keeps the bedroom warm. That helps. But I still sleep as you suggested with four pillows.'

I've been thinking how the initial sexual act with a virgin can be a perilous prelude to a marriage. A minority of women seem to feel animosity to the men who have deflowered them. It's not simply the fact that the first penetrative act does not fulfil the bride's expectations – something more puzzling than that, more mysterious.

Indeed, according to reports by some travellers and missionaries, the act of defloration in certain primitive tribes is denied the bridegroom in order to deflect any possible animosity. The hymen is ruptured by a husband surrogate – by the father of the bride or by the holy witch-doctor. Thereafter, a successful sexual marital relationship ensues. Certainly, numerous women, in my experience, apparently frigid and unhappy during their first marriage, after a divorce find happiness and sexual satisfaction in a second one.

After abstaining for a long time, I succumbed and masturbated late tonight, all the while keeping beautiful Yvonne Bloomberg in mind.

January 29th

I wrote a letter to Yvonne Bloomberg today. Simply, I thanked her for Söderberg's *Doctor Glas* and said how much I looked forward to reading it. Actually, I finished the novel last night. I can see myself in the author's portrait of Dr Glas, his views about euthanasia, his self-doubts, his attempt to seek some style in his unhappiness, his bachelorhood, his sense of undefined guilt. Glas writes a journal too. Then there is his passionate contempt for the ugly Rev. Gregorius and his infatuation with his wife. To be sure, I do not warm to the ugly Anton Bloomberg but I do not feel so passionately as all that. And yes, I do find his young wife diverting... But infatuation? No. No, no.

Before Rhys came round for our Sunday afternoon game of chess I stumbled on an old photograph album of my mother's. So many objects in this house remind me constantly of her: the pictures on the wall; that Persian rug she bought at an auction; that broken musical box that played 'Frère Jacques'. But these photographs and snapshots bring back, even more potently, half-forgotten things, adding a bitter lack to their sweet taste.

This photograph of Chekhov's study, his empty chair, I wonder what visitor to Russia had sent it to her long ago and why she had kept it. An admirer perhaps? Mother sometimes hinted that before she was married there had been another man in her life. I have a distinct memory of my parents arguing about the character of a certain timber merchant – my father denigrating him and my mother defending him, and how my father suddenly stamped out of the room. My mother seemed upset and when I asked her what a 'gigolo' was, she did not answer.

This sepia photograph of my father taken before I was born reveals unerringly his military bearing: his hair cut short, his moustache precise, his unsmiling countenance. Come to think of it, I can't ever recall my father laughing out loud. I think he must have always felt that my mother was in thraldom to my needs. 'You're spoiling the boy,' he would growl, 'you're smothering him.' 'He's all I've got,' she would reply tearfully.

My mother did pay me, perhaps, excessive attention when I returned from the hospital. During my convalescence my grouchy father rarely appeared in the house. When he did so he hardly spoke. He was silent at the dinner table and he was silent after dinner while mother tinkered in the kitchen. He would walk back and forth on the carpet near the fender, back and forth, back and forth, like a caged animal.

My firework accident parturated my fate. The hospital experience enticed me to become a doctor – that and my mother's later tuberculosis, her final illness. First, she had nursed me; at the last I nursed her. As one of Mrs Levy's sayings has it, 'When a parent gives to his son both laugh; when a son gives to the parent both cry.' My mother died, only fifty years of age.

And here's a fading snapshot of me when I was only so high. Those girlish curls! That sailor hat! The smiling figure behind me is Sybil, the maid. When once mother had a bout of influenza Sybil was detailed to bathe me. During that period when mother was confined to her bedroom, Sybil made a habit of tickling my small penis in the bath. It was our secret. When mother recovered I asked if Sybil could continue to bathe me. Soon after we had a different maid. 'Sybil had to go,' mother told me later. 'She used to pilfer things. I caught her red-handed with my amber brooch.'

One photo had not been stuck into the album. It is of my mother's grass-widowhood friend, Pamela Humphries. 'Aunt Pam,' I used to call her. When she moved to Newcastle I believe my mother missed her more than she ever did my father.

It is irksome that, generally, I remember my mother's visage not as in these smiling snapshots but as she forlornly stared back at me from her final pillow. In her terminal illness she frequently read the Bible. 'Shall I read you a page or two, mother?'

God is not a beautiful hypothesis but a necessary one.

In the middle of my second game with Rhys a phone call spirited me away from the living room. Hugh Fisher introduced himself: President of the Broadhurst Gardens Society. 'I'm so sorry I missed you at the Brains Trust,' he continued. 'Yvonne Bloomberg told me that you were most stimulating. She suggests you join our Society and that you may be particularly interested in our next meeting.'

'What . . . er?'

'We have a rabbi coming to talk about the legends of the Jews. Something we Christians need to know, don't you think? I'll send you details.'

When I returned I saw that Rhys had picked up *Doctor Glas*, which I had left on the coffee table.

'Any good?' he asked.

'It's about a doctor murdering someone.'

'Oh, not euthanasia again.'

'No, no. It is not a mercy killing.'

'I think if I were a doctor I'd be tempted to bump off someone sooner or later. Of course, I'd have to have a motive.'

'Why?' I asked. 'Why do criminals invent motives, reasons for killing someone? They kill because they need to kill and afterwards swipe the corpse's jewels or money. Otherwise they'd think themselves mad.'

'It's your move,' Rhys reminded me. 'Watch your queen or she's going to get murdered.'

That novel, the parallels! The fictitious Mrs Gregorius is young and beautiful and married to a repulsive older man whose sexual overtures she shrinks from. So it is with the young and beautiful

Mrs Bloomberg. Naturally, the frustrated Rev. Gregorius becomes agitated and seeks a doctor's advice. So, too, does the frustrated Mr Bloomberg.

In both cases what is good for the goose is bad for the gander. The dilemma? My patient is the gander, my concern is for the goose. So it was for Dr Glas.

One more note before I go to bed. Half an hour ago I tuned in to the Third Programme and heard not farts in different keys but Schoenberg's pantonal composition 'with twelve notes related to each other'. I turned the wireless off.

In hell, modern music is played ceaselessly, permanently.

And one more thought: if I painted the Devil, would I paint him nude?

February 3rd
However sceptical of medicine some patients consider themselves to be they are less resolute in their views at three o'clock in the morning when a scared light shines in their bedrooms. Ill, they long for a wizard to relieve them of their symptoms. Perforce, they surrender to his surrogate, the doctor, me, who bears no wand but a stethoscope.

So it was with old Jack Abbot. His cynicism proved soluble as soon as he experienced real pulmonary distress. It is wonderful that we doctors are now empowered with sulphonamides and penicillin and the new tetracycline drugs to arrest and defer so much human misery. Even tuberculosis, these days, can be defeated by streptomycin.

It is hardly any time at all since the crammed wards of hospitals seethed with patients suffering from festering wounds, pus-discharging abscesses, weeping fistulas, raw angry carbuncles. Ten years ago I had only nugatory power. Now, sometimes, I do feel that I possess a wand.

Because of a succession of pea-soup fogs I've been called out regularly to patients such as 'chesty' Jack Abbot. When I first examined him on Monday night I decided to travel by bus to St John's Wood because of the smog. The vehicle crawled along and when I alighted, carrying my little black bag, I almost lost my way. The Finchley Road was almost devoid of traffic and as I stumbled on, suddenly afflicted it seemed with double cataracts, I came across a baffled duck sitting on the pavement. Presumably it had wandered from Regent's Park and become disorientated. On my return journey, I observed a one-decker bus, destined for Edinburgh, being led by a man holding up a flare. A cartoon by Magritte.

Jack Abbot said to me, 'Old age is a mistake.'

February 4th

During my late dinner at the Cosmo, I was distracted from reading the *Evening Standard* with its news about a spy called Klaus Fuchs, by somebody singing in the adjacent annexe. Generally, the decibel level in that outpost of bohemia rises markedly. In contrast, the sparsely attended main section of the restaurant with its sober waiters, sedate linen tablecloths, and glittering heavy cutlery seemed as hushed as a bank. The fellow playing the guitar sang, 'Baby, it's cold outside'. It is a song frequently broadcast on the wireless these days but never had it seemed so apt. On the other side of the Cosmo's expansive plate-glass windows a freezing fog hovered in the diffused, pale-yellow lamplight.

I decided to order my coffee in the more cheerful, Dionysian annexe. Most of the small tables were occupied so I sat near the door on a comfortable, padded bench. At once the man next to me said in an unattractive, accented voice, 'Good evening, doctor.' I turned to meet the gaze of serious eyes behind excessively strong-lensed glasses.

'You don't know me,' he explained, 'but you treated my landlady, Mrs Burrows, when she had the shingles.'

He was a thick-set individual with a remarkably large head. His face was heavily jowled, his lips unnaturally loose. Possibly because of my own blemished features he felt a kinship with me. (I was sitting so that he could see the maroon scar on my cheek.) In consanguinity he soon informed me that during the war he'd earned his living as a chemist analysing milk for the United Dairies.

'I was not called up, of course.'

Because he was a refugee, I assumed, or perhaps because of a medical condition. Something about his features reminded me of some picture in a medical textbook. Anyway, his conversation was sprightly enough.

'And what are you doing now?' I asked.

'Oh,' he replied, 'I'm translating Shakespeare into German.'

More young people crowded into the annexe. Each time the door opened a blast of unwelcome ice-cold fog entered too. The tall, portly, imposing guitarist, who had overheard my companion remark that he was translating Shakespeare, strummed on the guitar for a few moments before giving a comical rendering of Hamlet's 'To be or not to be' as declaimed by a guttural-voiced German. He repeated the soliloquy, first imitating the accent of a Frenchman and then that of a Scandinavian to much laughter and applause. For an encore he sang conversationally:

When I was a teeny-tot
They put me on the wee-wee pot
To see if I could wee or not...

He paused significantly before adding, I COULD NOT. More laughter and I thought how pleasant it would be if Yvonne Bloomberg happened to come into the café. In the menace of the present weather, her husband, because of his dodgy chest, would be forced to stay indoors.

Then somebody named Kevin called on the translator of Shakespeare to perform his party trick. 'Come on, Erich,' they all jubilated in unison. Amongst the youthful company I certainly felt the age in my mouth. I was very much a spectator. Erich, next to me, stood up and everybody cheered. He walked with a strange ataxic gait, suggesting he had a congenital condition. At the far wall he deliberately cracked his large head against it resoundingly several times. Applause followed but he then lurched out of the restaurant as if offended. For half a minute those at the tables became tamed and quiet. It occurred to me that Erich had that medical condition, Friedrich's ataxy, hence his clumsy gait and, presumably, the thickened bone of his skull which allowed him to assault the wall with it.

Soon the party atmosphere returned and the guitarist began to sing again. I observed one young couple at a table with arms about each other, the fellow's hand almost cupping her breast. She smiled up at him in unmitigated adoration and I recalled – approximately – some lines of Walt Whitman: 'When I peruse the fame of heroes and the victories of mighty generals, I do not envy the generals nor the President in his Presidency, nor the rich in their great houses, but when I hear of lovers, unfalteringly together, I hastily walk away filled with the bitterest envy.'

If, during the evening, those in the annexe seemed to behave more boisterously than usual, their inhibitions released, could it have been because of the fog outside that abolished the juridical world, deleted each highway and byway, each cul de sac, each familiar building and street? I left the warmth of the Cosmo annexe and entered the cold of a suddenly alien country.

February 7th
The fogs have gone. This is croup weather. Colds and croup. The older I get the more I long for summer. I see myself sitting on a

park bench watching, leisurely, the highest, jubilant, sunlit, silver point of a fountain.

February 12th

Saturday night, at the Broadhurst Gardens Centre I sat next to Mrs Levy. Yvonne Bloomberg occupied the seat in front of me. I arrived after the meeting had commenced and, as I settled myself in the wooden chair, trying to make no more noise than an ant, she turned round to smile at me sweetly. On the raised platform, to the right of the lectern, sat the chairman, Hugh Fisher. And at the lectern itself, the rabbi, a bespectacled, balding man, held forth, his hands never still. He raised high both his arms at intervals, as if he had a threatening gun pressed in his back. He was not, as I had expected, one of those grotesque bearded rabbis dressed in ridiculous clothes. I lost the drift of his talk at one point, having been distracted by the exquisite hairline at the back of Yvonne Bloomberg's neck. What would have happened, I had been wondering, if I had leant forward impulsively to kiss the skin below her curls as gently as butterfly wings?

'He's got a voice that creaks,' Mrs Levy whispered to me.

'What?'

'His voice. It needs oiling. It creaks.'

Evidently the rabbi had lost Mrs Levy also. I tried to focus again on what he was saying. 'Those thirteenth-century kabbalists strove to transform Judaism into a mystery religion. But to return to the legends...'

'Wait long enough and gossip becomes a legend,' Mrs Levy whispered.

I nodded but someone behind me, some irritable bugger, hoarsely uttered, 'Hush.'

Castigated, hoping that Yvonne Bloomberg hadn't overheard the small rumpus, I firmly directed my gaze towards the platform. Hugh Fisher was making notes, presumably for the vote of thanks. He wore a polo-neck, knitted sweater. Quite young. Only thirty, maximum. A school teacher? Audience laughter suddenly woke me up. The rabbi beamed. 'Yes, and when those fallen angels observed how beautiful were the daughters of men they lusted after them and begat children.'

'It was before Marie Stopes,' Mrs Levy irrepressibly whispered to me.

'The virgin, Naamah, was but one who led the angels astray by her beauty,' the rabbi continued. 'According to legend, once those angels descended to earth they lost their transcendental qualities and could procreate with women.'

I could not see Yvonne Bloomberg's expression. She sat there, motionless, rapt. Again, ridiculously, I wondered whether she was the angel-like schoolgirl of Netherhall Gardens.

At the conclusion of the meeting a number of the audience stayed behind for coffee and social chat. I guessed half of them were Jewish. Some I had seen in the cosmopolitan cafés or in the Swiss Cottage pub. The loquacious Mrs Levy collared me. 'Do you know the story, doctor, of Mr Cohen when his wife was almost kaput? He asked God to send only a lazy messenger to alert the Angel of Death...Ah...' she interrupted herself, 'there's my husband coming in. He's later than usual. He usually contrives cleverly to come in time for the vote of thanks.'

Yvonne stood near the raised platform in conversation with gawky Hugh Fisher. I ambled over to them. Together they persuaded me to give a future talk at the Society about new trends in medicine. 'All proceeds,' added Fisher, 'go to charity.' I learnt that he worked in the accounts department of the BBC. When I remarked that I found the rabbi's magisterial discussion about angels fascinating I noted Yvonne's enigmatic, archaic smile. As for Hugh Fisher, because his hair has begun to recede and his eyebrows have grown too high on his forehead, he resembles a lachrymose clown, perpetually perplexed.

'Can I give you a lift?' I asked Yvonne Bloomberg. 'I pass your place on my way home. My car is parked outside.'

'I hear they're going to end petrol rationing soon,' said Fisher. 'Another promise now that Attlee's got the election in a couple of weeks.'

Instead of driving straight up the incline of tree-lined Fitzjohn's Avenue, I impulsively made a detour so that we would pass through Netherhall Gardens. I had not planned this absurd peregrination and she did not redirect me. In Maresfield Gardens, slowing down and changing into second gear, I pointed to where Sigmund Freud had lived before he died eleven years ago.

'One more tragic, Swiss Cottage refugee,' said Yvonne Bloomberg. Then added: 'In April, in that front garden, one can see a magnificent, a matchless almond tree in blossom.'

Evidently she was familiar with these calm suburban roads. Netherhall Gardens was but minutes away.

'Just before the war, at a BMA meeting,' I reminisced, 'I met Dr Harmer, one of Freud's physicians during his last year. Harmer told me that when Freud had been buttonholed by a rapacious, ardent Marxist, Freud stated that he'd been half-converted. The communist argued that the dictatorship of the proletariat would lead to years of misery but that universal prosperity and happiness would follow. Freud teased that he definitely believed the first half.'

We both laughed. That was the first time we seemed so in accord. As we passed the obscure house in Netherhall Gardens, she meditated, 'Dr Harmer. That's a helluva name for a physician.'

The house looked far from welcoming. A light in the hall dimly diffused through the denying glass of the front door. Almost immediately we reached the end of the road and rejoined Fitzjohn's Avenue. At the traffic lights, near the Everyman Cinema, I turned right down Rosslyn Hill.

Some minutes later I swivelled into the road I was looking for. I could see ahead the 1930s block of luxury apartments with its scatter of lit windows where the Bloombergs lived. I parked near a house that had been cross-sectioned during an air-raid. Its stairs, in the semi-darkness, climbed up to nowhere.

'I enjoyed reading the *Dr Glas* book,' I said. 'Does it in some way reflect your experience?'

'How do you mean?' she replied, suddenly glacial.

I said nothing. I had been too impetuous.

'You mean my marriage?'

Having gone so far I decided to dare more. 'I hope it's better now that you're not sharing the bedroom.'

'Of course we share the bedroom. You don't think Anton would sleep in the guest room, do you?' She turned to glare at me with latent hostility. 'Is this a consultation, doctor?'

'Please,' I said and touched her shoulder.

Suddenly she began to sob. I let my hand rest there and said, 'I'm sorry.' I was so aware of her physical presence. She seemed both seductively bewitching and paradoxically unblemished. She searched for a handkerchief in her handbag and stammered, 'I'm sorry, doctor.'

'Those who know me well call me Robbie,' I said.

Soon she became calm and told me how a few nights earlier her husband had sadistically tried to rape her. 'He tried to turn me over and take me from behind,' she said softly. Then, as if breaking out of a cage, she opened the car door and without one further word, neither a 'thank you' nor a 'goodbye' walked rapidly towards the high block of flats.

I drove home thinking that, like the beautiful Naamah the rabbi spoke about, Yvonne Bloomberg, too, would have carnally tempted the most recalcitrant of celestial creatures.

February 13th

I keep going over Saturday night's churlish conversation in the car. How could I have probed like that? Yvonne did not know her husband had consulted me. My words, blundering, had hurt her. I can't erase them.

How innocent is she? To have married an unattractive older man like that must have been financially rewarding, must have allowed her economic security. That export-import business with the vast showrooms in Great Portland Street, which Bloomberg bragged about in my surgery, must have provided him with Croesus money. Presumably, when she was knocking around regularly with the clientele of the Cosmo annexe before Bloomberg came on the scene less than a year ago, she probably had little spare cash. From one shabby, rented room to that luxury Hampstead apartment would have been quite a graduation. Of course, I don't know where she lived prior to her marriage. Netherhall Gardens? Hardly. She could have been living in a doss house for all I know. Yet she was as smartly dressed, as well-groomed as she is now.

But the sudden weeping episode in my car, was that mere play-acting? Or did I provoke genuine tears? Could she have been influenced by the novel she has given me? In an early chapter, the heroine, Mrs Gregorius, the young Mrs Gregorius, married to an odious older man, commands Dr Glas's sympathy and help by breaking down and crying. I have the book here on the desk in front of me: 'Mrs Gregorius sank down on a chair shaken with weeping ... I [Dr Glas] went over to her, took her hand, patted it slowly. There, there, don't cry any more now. I'll help you, I promise.'

And Dr Glas kept his promise by poisoning her husband! Well, I'm not Dr Glas. I don't carry sodium cyanide in my pocket.

I'm startled. After I wrote the above in my journal I flicked through the pages of Söderberg's novel. It's eerie. I had forgotten. Dr Glas, in his initial attempt to aid his attractive young patient, tells the Rev. Gregorius that because of his heart condition it would be hazardous for him to sleep with his wife. He says, imperiously, 'My prescription is clear and simple: it reads "separate bedrooms"... I don't think I'm exceeding the bounds of what is reasonable if I point out that the constant propinquity of a young woman, particularly at night, must have much the same effect on a clergyman as on any other mortal man...'

I had not read that detail in the novel when Bloomberg consulted me a few weeks ago, yet I, also, had prescribed separate bedrooms. My advice was offered in order to help Anton Bloomberg. Or was it? In any case, Dr Glas had more authority over his patient than me. Bloomberg did not take my advice.

February 14th

A home-made Valentine card. Within a 'heart' shape, drawn in red ink, a pathetic quatrain:

> Robert, you shall find your love
> And I shall tell you why.
> For you are a filthy pig
> Who shits within your sty.

The handwriting very small. Surely the same sick person who wrote me care of the *Hampstead and Highgate Express* and who held forth about the evil in the world. A local postmark on the envelope. A patient or ex-patient perhaps? Someone evidently antagonistic to me. Some patients never forgive doctors who have helped them. There is such a thing as the sin of gratitude.

This person, though, could be completely off his head. I have encountered many in my practice over the years, suffering paranoid delusions or with megalomaniacal ideas of grandeur. To see such a stricken patient recover, after all the moans and shrieks, is like watching the glory of a baby being born.

I listened to an interesting talk on the Third Programme by Michael S. Parr. About love and marriage – presumably because it is St Valentine's Day. I enjoyed the insightful offerings of the celebrated – extracts from letters and poems interspersed with popular musical pieces chosen because of their lyrics. The latter seemed almost exclusively about loss, among them my favourites like 'These Foolish Things' and 'Thanks for the Memory'. It was all blue and sentimental and winsome. Parr presented those waxing for marriage and those against it. Richard Burton was quoted – I've looked up the exact extract since – 'Tis a hazard both ways I confess to live simple or to marry. *Nam et uxorem ducere et non ducere malum est*, it may be bad, it may be good, as it is a cross and calamity on the one side, so 'tis a secret delight, an incomparable happiness, a blessed estate, a most unspeakable benefit, a sole content, on the other...' For my mother I believe it was the former: a cross and a calamity.

I was listening to Michael Parr discussing how St Paul had recommended marriage while he, himself, led the single life when I was called to the telephone.

'Who?'

'Frank Middleton.'

'Who?'

'Frank Middleton. We met you at the Blue Danube with Rhys.'

'Oh yes, of course.'

To my surprise he invited me to a dinner party at his home in Richmond a week next Saturday. I accepted hurriedly because I wished to resume listening to the wireless. I got back to hear the actor speak lines by P.G. Wodehouse: 'I was in rare fettle and the heart had touched a new high. I don't know anything that braces one up like finding you haven't got to get married after all.'

I shall be forty on March 17th. I'm not likely to get married now. I'm not Anton Bloomberg lusting after a young girl. I don't think I could bear living with someone closely, not every day, 24 hours round, a carousel of days and nights, sharing the bedroom, the bathroom, the lav, everything. No. No, thank you. Edith, my meticulous, maternal Edith, takes care of me well enough. Ever since she became a widow she has come in early enough to supervise the daily help, to act as a filter when thrusting patients attempt to reach me, to regulate each queachy detail. When I'm on my afternoon rounds she sits contentedly in the kitchen next to the big stove, pondering my *Manchester Guardian*'s crossword puzzle. She doesn't have to stay for my evening surgery, though she generally lingers on before taking the Northern Line Tube back to her place in Hendon.

I wish I hadn't accepted Frank Middleton's invitation. Rhys said his wife was entranced by doctors. Too many people have a morbid interest in medicine. They read all those doctor columns in the popular press and afterwards examine their faeces in the morning lavatory bowl. I bet Mrs Middleton – Amy Middleton – will invite another doctor to her table. That means the conversation over dinner will be about the National Health Service again. Oh dear. And having to go out to Richmond where they live – that's a drag.

February 17th
Some patients, honestly:
    Mrs Harvey: I understand it's possible to catch polio from a budgerigar.
    Me: Why do you ask?
    Mrs Harvey: I heard it's possible or is it a rumour?
    Me: Is your budgerigar sick?
    Mrs Harvey: I haven't got a budgerigar.
    Me: You haven't got a budgerigar?
    Mrs Harvey: No, doctor.
    Me: Then you've got nothing to worry about.
    Mrs Harvey: My niece wants a budgerigar. I don't want to give her anything dangerous.
    By contrast my next patient happened to be Colin Stant. Before the war he had been a brilliant young cricket player destined to bat not only for Middlesex but probably for England

too. But his eyes had been ruined by being a prisoner of war, starved by the Japanese.

When I first saw him, because of his prolonged deficiency of Vitamin A, I prescribed large doses of that vitamin. At least the skin lesions he suffered from – rough, dry skin resembling goose flesh – responded to treatment.

I sometimes ponder on his almost incredible war story: how after being taken prisoner in the Far East, eventually in 1945, he, along with many others, was shipped back to Japan. But, near the Japanese coast, the ship was torpedoed. Struggling in the sea, holding on to a heaving piece of wreckage, he was one of some survivors picked up by a Japanese fishing boat. Fished out of the water they were then taken back to the nearest Japanese port – Nagasaki.

Colin reckons the atom bomb saved his life! He was being forced to dig a trench for his own grave when the prisoners and guards heard the drone of an aeroplane coming nearer and nearer.

February 19th

Rhys has become a Francophile. It's the books he buys from Zwemmer's in Charing Cross Road, the plays he sees in the West End or at the Embassy in Swiss Cottage, the films at the Everyman around the corner. It's Camus and Anouilh, Cocteau and Sartre. This afternoon he even favoured the French defence in our chess game! And afterwards he dished up some existentialist arguments. Rhys seems to be suggesting that thinking men can be free to choose and thus they have the life they deserve.

'You think I have the life I deserve?' I asked him.

'Yes, you have,' Rhys replied.

I showed him my deformed hand. And I thought of my sick patients. Did they choose their illnesses?

'Yes, I think they do,' Rhys said stubbornly. 'Our lives are like these chess games of ours, absurd. One chooses this, one chooses that. It's equally absurd.'

'Our refugee friends, did they choose to be Jews? The Chosen People! Joke! No, our chromosomes do the choosing for us.'

'You don't face up to it, Robbie,' argued Rhys. 'We live our lives most of the time asleep or thought-sedated. Because of a dread that we can't define our lives are absurd. Certainly there's no point to my life. That's why this coming week I'm going to buy a television set! My choice!'

Rhys doesn't work. He just collects rents on Fridays. He has too much leisure.

February 20th

I wish Rachel Butler would allow me to arrange some nursing help for her. She looks so worn, weary. She waits on him hand and foot and heart and head. She has a neighbour, an ex-nurse, who comes in sometimes. An RAMC nurse, not that long demobilised. 'You should take advantage of that,' I said, 'and go out sometimes. To the theatre or something.'

'I don't like to leave him,' she replied. 'If I did so I wouldn't enjoy myself. I'd worry about Michael.'

She doesn't want any help. By being a slave to her husband it is as if she is making reparation for something I don't know about. When I gave the morphine jab to her husband, as usual he spoke with assumed gusto. I told him that he should persuade his wife to go out some time.

'She goes out to shop in the morning,' Michael Butler said.

'There's a good film at the Everyman I hear – *The Battleship Potemkin*,' I said. 'A Russian film.'

'I don't keep her in chains, doctor,' he said. Maybe not, I thought, but she has put herself in chains.

Michael Butler changed the subject as quickly as he could and told me a story about General Potemkin. It was a kind of parable but I couldn't see the point of it. I could not see what lesson it taught. It continues to puzzle me. All I know is that Michael Butler is a fine story-teller.

When Potemkin experienced one of his episodes of depression no one, not even those of the highest rank, were allowed to go near him. He stayed in his room with the door shut. Documents piled up awaiting the General's signature. The Empress insisted that the General should sign them. The top civil servants were afraid to approach him. At last, the humble clerk Shuvalkin, to the amazement of all, took the sheaf of documents, head high in the air. He's for the chop, they all said.

After traversing the long corridors and the marble stairs, Shuvalkin finally arrives at the General's room and enters it without even knocking. The curtains are drawn. The General sits at his desk, head in hands. The lowly clerk takes a pen, dips it in the ink and gives it to the General who stares at him for a moment. Shuvalkin then places the documents before him and, as if in a dream, the General signs one document after the other. No word is spoken.

All the documents signed, Shuvalkin quits the room, closes the heavy carved door, descends the wide marble staircase, threads his way down the long galleries and corridors until at last he reaches the vast and airy councillors' room.

'There,' the clerk exclaims triumphantly, throwing the documents on to the massive, highly-polished conference table. 'They are all signed.'

The councillors, amazed, advance to the table. They examine the papers. Soon, they all look up from the table towards the proud clerk. They have odd, unsmiling expressions on their faces. They have perceived that each document, one after the other, bears the signature Shuvalkin, Shuvalkin, Shuvalkin, Shuvalkin...

When I returned home after my afternoon rounds I asked Edith, as is my custom, if there were any messages. She stood there, smirking, irritating me as she told me Mrs Bloomberg had called. 'I think it was a social visit,' said Edith knowingly. 'Her husband is a patient of ours.'

'What did she say?' I asked, ignoring the innuendo manifest in her posture and tone of voice.

'She just asked me to say that she was sorry about the other evening and that she will be in touch with you.'

I could sense that Edith was very curious. 'Ours,' she had said, 'a patient of ours.' She has a proprietary interest in all my patients. She tends to claim them for herself, as if they had consulted her and she had diagnosed their symptoms, written out their prescriptions. On the other hand, she is very protective of me. In any case, what does it matter? I feel as light as helium. Yvonne Bloomberg had surely come to me for help. The apology was mere subterfuge, for what had she to apologise for?

'She was wearing too much perfume, that Mrs Bloomberg,' Edith grumpily complained, and turned away towards her patch in the warm kitchen.

How can I help Yvonne adroitly? She is very young and vulnerable. What advice can I confidently give her? There are grounds surely for her to seek a divorce. She has only been married a few months. It's hardly any time at all since she stood in Hampstead Registry Office, next to Anton Bloomberg and said, 'I will,' and swore to obey and serve him, love, honour, and keep him in sickness and in health.

His physical brutality. But divorce takes such a long time and is not easy. One hears of fictional adultery arrangements at an hotel, a messy set-up with a hired private detective as witness. All so seedy. I can imagine myself in bed with her, the detective breaking in, my arm about her protectively, her bare breasts, and the impertinent flash of a photograph being taken. I would not like to be cited as a co-respondent: the danger of being struck off the Medical Register. Besides, she may not wish to be separated from the fellow, perhaps she wishes to honour the oath made in the Registry Office. And apart from anything else, she is probably economically dependent on his largesse. 'And forsaking all other, keep thee only unto him, so long as you both shall live.'

Anyway, what business is it of mine? Let go, let go.

After dinner, ridiculously, compulsively, I drove to that tower block of luxurious flats close to the bombed, derelict house. I parked the car, turned off the headlights, and smoked a cigarette. I could not think of an excuse which sounded authentic enough for me to call on the Bloombergs. Up there, behind the curtains of one of those lit windows presumably they were together. I recalled something Rhys once remarked: 'Women don't marry for money, they simply make sure to fall in love with rich men.' I threw the dibby out of the car window and drove home, no longer feeling helium-light.

February 21st
I woke up in the middle of the night. I had dreamt in colours, vivid gaudy colours. I was holding the hand of my father and I was looking at that hand. It had hair on it. We gazed up together at rockets which were bursting in the night sky. I saw clearly fountains of fire, green and blue, red and yellow, streaks of silvery threads, trickling down, falling, falling. It must have been Guy Fawkes night.

'Penny for the guy, penny for the guy,' a child was shouting. As I drew near, I saw a life-size dummy dressed in dark clothes – it owned the white-as-chalk face of Anton Bloomberg. 'Burn, burn,' a child was shouting. Suddenly the dummy was being carried through the streets and I joined the procession. People were shouting, 'Burn, burn.' And when the dummy was thrown on to the bonfire I saw, amidst the swirling smoke and the leaping crimson and gold flames, my own pitiful face burning,

not Bloomberg's, and my eyes staring back in horror at me.
Each night we enter the lunatic asylum of Sleep.

I keep imagining venal love between Anton and Yvonne
Bloomberg. I see them in different sexual positions. Why do I
keep tormenting myself? Why do I feel everything is
provisional?

February 26th
When I awoke this morning a band of sunlight barged through
the partially drawn curtains. I could hear the distant church bells
pleasantly proclaiming it was Sunday morning. Still somnolent,
I thought momentarily of serious sabbaths when, as a boy, I
accompanied my mother to church. Eyes closed, I conjured up
the chiaroscuro shadows in the half-filled pews, the small plump
cushions, the coffin-black prayer books with their trailing
ribbons, the contrasting brightness in the church's coloured glass
windows. I used to enjoy the old togetherness of singing hymns
and even responded to the earnest sound of the organ. I fell
asleep again. When I woke up and heard the sermon of the small
clock on my bedside table, I saw that it was almost lunchtime.
Then I remembered what had happened last night.

I got out of bed. The bedroom air was stale. I pulled back the
curtains, opened the window wide. It was all sunlight that made
my sleepy eyes crinkle, bird-whistle and an infusion of
springtime-loaded air. Across the road the smoke wandered from
the chimney pots and Mr Bailey was taking down the election
poster he had put up. On Friday, Labour had won the election.
Just! Attlee was back in power but it was the closest result for a
hundred years. The Tories, of course, had retained Hampstead.

Looking down to our front garden I could see the first
crocuses. Not far away, on the Heath, foxes would be mating and
the Great Crested Grebes would be returning to the Hampstead

ponds. As I stood there, by the curtains, I heard so many birds in rapturous song.

It was not like that last night when, sanguine, I left – somewhat late – for my dinner date. What had been a mild mist in Hampstead matured into a blatant fog halfway round the North Circular Road. The muzzled lights of oncoming cars, the other side of the road, stealthily parted and scattered the rolling fog and I had to drive slowly. I would have considered turning back but I reflected that Amy Middleton would have taken time to prepare a meal and that she and her husband, apart from other guests – probably based more locally – would be waiting for me. At Kew Bridge, the traffic, half-blinded, had slowed to a crawl while, invisibly, beneath the bridge, the Thames flowed on.

Worse, in Richmond itself, I lost my way. I had turned into the wrong suburban road – into Arcadia Way, not Arcadia Road. I knew I was quite near but there were no pedestrians about to give me directions. I saw just ahead a detached house, lights in every window and acoustically loud with music. Someone celebrating the election result? I stopped the car opposite and decided to knock on the door, explain and ask. As I crossed the road I heard a tiny cry near my feet. A kitten, not much bigger than my hand. I couldn't leave it there. It belonged, presumably, to somebody who lived in one of these houses.

I had to bang hard several times on the front door of the house. The raised voices within, the laughter, the loud music, reminded me of parties of my youth and how I had felt that if it hadn't been for my facial scar nobody would notice me. At last the door opened and a bubbly girl, seeing me with a kitten in my arms, almost screamed, 'What a dainty present! I'll get Thelma. She'll be thrilled.' She swiftly disappeared into one of the rooms. Two men were leaning on the wall in the hallway and I heard one remark, 'History is so depressing.' I waited for a pause in the conversation before asking if they could direct me to Arcadia Road.

'Jim will know.' One of them pointed to a young man sitting on the stairs talking to a girl with red hair wearing a blue dress.

'Go down to the end of the road,' I was told, 'turn right, then left and you're there.'

The bubbly girl returned with Thelma who, I had already discovered, was celebrating her 21st birthday. She looked at me searchingly as if for something she did not want to find. Impulsively, I handed the kitten to her. She said a doubtful, puzzled, thank you, and suggested that I take off my overcoat and join the party. I was tempted to stay, if only for one drink, but it was already past nine o'clock and the Middleton dinner had been arranged for eight.

I drove away as 'Jim' had directed, all the while thinking about the kitten. Would some irate neighbour tomorrow or the next day claim the 'dinky' creature from Thelma. I had a story to relate at the Middleton dinner table! I hoped Frank Middleton had a sense of humour.

When I arrived, though, no Frank was to be seen, no guests either.

'Have I got the wrong Saturday?' I asked.

'No, no,' said Amy Middleton. 'I've been expecting you. Frank had to go to Germany. So I didn't ask anybody else. I'm just putting Sylvia to bed. I won't be long. I expect you're very hungry.'

Between chess games I regaled Rhys with a little of what had happened last night: how, following dinner and coffee, Amy had, in meaningful tones, insisted that, given the foggy weather, I stay the night. I had prevaricated and she had added, laughing, 'You can borrow Frank's pyjamas.'

'You lucky dab,' commented Rhys. And then vulgarly grunted, 'She must have been a good variegated fuck. She's the right vintage.'

His remarks did not encourage me to elaborate. I changed the subject and asked Rhys what he thought about the election results. He jabbered on about how Churchill was correct, that since Attlee had only a single figure majority there'd be another election before long.

'It's a lame duck government,' opined Rhys. 'One tantrum and they're out.'

What happened last night I can more easily relate here in my journal rather than articulating it in detail out loud to Rhys. Amy Middleton did persuade me to stay. 'I'll make up a bed in the spare room.' But she hinted that she would welcome a nocturnal visit from me. 'I keep my bedroom door open in case Sylvia should shout – though she never does.'

My shuffling into one bedroom and she into another had been merely decorous play-acting. I reclined in the darkness of the guest room knowing full well she expected me to cross the landing corridor. I did not dither too long. It was like being offered delicious strawberries and cream when you're not hungry. You eat them up nevertheless.

I felt incapacitated by the fact that I was wearing her husband's pyjamas. When I lay in bed with her she asked me, after a groping minute, what was wrong? I blamed the pyjamas and she said directly, 'Well, why don't you take the tops off too?' As I write this I realise that the situation might sound comical. It was not so. Not for me. It was over almost as soon as it began. 'I'm sorry,' I said. She stroked my hair and said, 'Don't worry. That's just a whiff. Next time, love, it'll be better.'

I couldn't sleep next to her. I wanted to get away without being impolite. I was so restless, she must have guessed. Finally she fell asleep. At two o'clock I tiptoed from the bedroom, got dressed, left the house furtively like a burglar and, discovering that the fog had become less dense, drove home.

February 27th
I dreamt I was striving so hard and had journeyed so far. I skirted precipitous chasms, azoic rock masses, primordial ridges and slopes to reach finally only a frosted window.

I was taught about diseases, not about patients. How can a doctor function without reverence?

This evening in the Cosmo annexe. At one table a group of mainly young people were talking about reincarnation. A moustached man of an older generation remarked with some passion – I could hear him clearly – that when you scrutinise a cat or a dog or an animal in the zoo closely, minutely, like an artist about to make a drawing, you can see within that creature a human being looking back at you mockingly.

I think all animals are mad.

February 28th
Phone-call from Rhys. A party. Would I care to join him tomorrow night at the London Welsh Club. 'St David's Day. It'll be quite a thrash. They'll roll out a barrel of beer as big as the Tower of Pisa and there'll be such singing it'll frighten the life into you. Frank and Amy Middleton are coming. So I thought you might join us for a Smith's Crisp.'

'You've invited Frank and Amy Middleton?'

'Do come, Robbie. It'll be heart-breaking harps, hwyl and hiraeth.'

'Frank Middleton's back from Germany?'

I declined. I had taken flight from that house in Richmond. I didn't want to be reminded of the fiasco by spending an evening of fake jollity and togetherness with Amy Middleton and her (I suspect) regularly cuckolded husband. Whoever said – was it Rhys? – 'Better to stay up all night and talk than to go to bed with a dragon,' was damn right.

The specialist at the Middlesex Hospital has confirmed that young Colin Wharton has leukaemia. I had to inform Mrs Wharton and she cried out, 'Why my Colin, my innocent Colin? What wrong has he ever done?' Despite rationality, despite the

76

parable of Job that surely teaches us that the sun shines down indiscriminately on the good and bad alike, deep down, in the innermost recesses of our beings, beyond all conscious thought, we view illness like we do ugly appearance, as the visible suppuration of sin, personal or familial.

We feel somewhat similarly about the Jews. Are they not the sons and daughters of Ahasuerus who, in medieval legend, was cursed because he refused our Lord rest at his door when he bore his cross to Calvary?

So Frank Middleton's back. For how long? How embarrassing an evening would it have been for me if I had agreed to go to the St David's Day party? Rhys will be in his element. Despite his confident, plummy English accent – he had elocution lessons when he was a boy – he is very conscious of being Welsh. He even looks Welsh: the wide brow; his hair black as shoe polish; his dark, sunken, watchful, brown eyes; and small red mouth. And he is short-statured, as many Welshmen are.

'It's not genetics,' he once argued, 'it's centuries of preposterous English oppression. They did for us in the femurs, boy – the malnutrition, the slave-diet so that we'd fit into their colliery tunnels. Anyhow, as Lloyd George asserted, in Wales we measure people from the neck up.'

I do not think Rhys's anti-English remarks are always sincere yet his stated belief – he's said it often enough – that he belongs to a defeated nation is deeply felt. Despite all his bragging and bluster he has an inferiority complex about being Welsh. He displays an ambivalence about his Welsh identity. I've heard him raise up high the Welsh flag, proud to march under it, but within an hour he will savage the character of his fellow-countrymen. 'We're cunning and boastful,' he'll argue. 'We may have the gift of the gab but our verbal exuberance leads us over the top into unintentional comedy. Listen, Robbie, when Shakespeare portrayed Owain Glyndwr, do you remember how our great

Prince swanked, thumbs in his braces, if he had 'em, "At my birth, the front of heaven was full of fiery shapes. The goats ran from the mountains and the herds went strangely clamorous to the frighted fields. These signs have marked me extraordinary and all the courses of my life do show I'm not in the roll of common men." Shakespeare, that Englishman, was laughing at us, boy. Justifiably.'

When I applauded the fact that he spoke these lines of Shakespeare with such facility, he replied in an assumed though authentic Welsh accent, 'Yeh, mun, I'm a bit of a dab 'and at it,' and exploded into laughter, mocking himself. Then he added soberly, 'The buggers cast me as Glyndwr in the school play. I can call spirits, Robbie boy, from the vasty deep.'

March 1st

Bloomberg came into my surgery this morning. At first, he hardly mentioned Yvonne. He was more concerned about his asthma, which had been troubling him again at night. 'It's come back,' he complained, 'ever since I heard my sister in Stockholm is seriously ill. I expect it's psychological – but knowing that doesn't help.'

I examined him on my black leather couch. He reclined back, shirt and vest removed, defenceless, his eyes wide, as I requested him to breathe in, to breathe out. I heard through my stethoscope the little cries and weeping of his bronchial tubes, the rales and rhonchi, and I remembered his young wife's cry for help.

I had read recently, in a medical journal, how twelve asthmatics had been treated with daily subcutaneous injections of vitamin B_{12} for fifteen to twenty days. In ten of these cases it was reported that their asthmatic attacks subsequently decreased or disappeared. The patients' general condition improved, they gained in weight and confessed to a feeling of well-being.

'Would you like to try it?' I said. 'I don't guarantee anything.'

'A daily injection, coming here?'

'Yes.'

'All right. It's not very convenient,' he grumbled, as if he were doing me a favour. 'I'll have to ask Yvonne to keep an eye on our Portland Street place.'

As he put his vest and shirt back on I learnt from him something of the prolegomenon to what seems to be their disastrous marriage. Tim Roberts had owned the business and had employed Bloomberg, at first a grateful dependent refugee who, through his industry and knowledge of foreign languages, had been promoted until he became Roberts's indispensable right-hand man.

When Tim Roberts had suffered a coronary and died, he, Anton Bloomberg, had taken charge of the firm on Yvonne Roberts's behalf. Yvonne was the sole heir – her mother, before the war, had not survived her second pregnancy and the baby had also been lost. 'If it wasn't for me,' boasted Bloomberg, 'the whole guesheft would have gone down the pan.'

The more I heard about their export-import business the more I realised they were bound together not only by the law of England, the ceremonial oaths of marriage, but most powerfully by the secure handcuffs of finance. 'Poor Yvonne,' I thought, 'she must feel trapped, in need of advice from some Houdini.'

Anton Bloomberg, now fully dressed, was ready to leave. I told him that we could start the daily injection next week. 'Meanwhile,' I explained, 'I'm going to prescribe tetracycline tablets for you. You have a low-grade infection in your tubes, which is not helping your asthma.'

He waited, standing much too close to me while I wrote out the prescription. Afterwards he said, 'Thank you,' and held out his hand. I took it, as I had to, aware of my deformity and feeling as if I were disloyal to Yvonne at the same time.

I've been reflecting on how much I have misjudged Yvonne. She had not married him for money. On the contrary, he had probably married her so that he could take over her father's business completely. That she was beautiful, young, was of course no hindrance as far as he was concerned. But surely it wasn't a love match? Surely it was a marriage of convenience? Even if that is not the truth of the matter, that is the meaning of the matter.

I wonder how much love existed between my mother and father. Had he wedded mother because of my grandparents' wealth? Mother, of course, was bereft when he left. She told me so often enough, yet she never rhapsodised about the early, possibly loving, years of her marriage. She thrived as a grass widow however much she complained. As we both grew older she depended as much on me as I had done on her.

Bloomberg. I really don't like him. There is something repugnant about the man. I understand how Dr Glas felt about the Rev. Gregorius. In treating Anton Bloomberg I need to remember my Hippocratic oath: 'I swear by Apollo the healer and Asclepius and Hygeia and all the gods and goddesses that I will follow that system of regimen which according to my ability and judgement I consider for the benefit of my patients, and abstain from whatever is deleterious and mischievous. I will give no deadly medicines to anyone ... etc. etc.'

It seems such a long time since I passed my final examinations. In that old building in Queens Square, here in London, after being congratulated by severe-looking men in severe suits – among them my examiners – I signed so lightly the Hippocratic oath. At last I had been given the licence that I had longed for. I remember the pleasure the passing of my Finals had given my mother, her pride in me and how pleased I myself had been on hearing people, for the first time, call me 'Doctor'. I had found it odd to be thus addressed. Now I find it odd if I am called 'Mr'.

How different it was then: the whole of my medical education had emphasised the importance of diagnosis rather than treatment. It could not have been otherwise because the discovery of antibiotics and the consequent therapeutic revolution had not taken place. The time-worn prescriptions I wrote out when I first qualified were pragmatic or simply magical. (Perhaps I'll talk on such matters when I lecture, or rather chat, at the Broadhurst Gardens Centre.) Now, today, I write out prescriptions for specific drugs which can combat specific diseases. I do not forget, though, what I was taught at the Westminster Hospital Medical School – that 18th-century imperative:

Be not the first by whom the new are tried,
Nor yet the last to lay the old aside.

March 2nd
When I was having breakfast this morning I observed two blackbirds through the window. They faced each other, hardly moving for a while, hypnotising each other it would seem, one with yellow beak lifted high, its tail low and fanned. At last one flew to the roof of the woodshed and the other immediately followed. Again they seemed to stare each other out. Up they went together, arising from the woodshed roof, both to land simultaneously, like expert acrobats, on the garden wall. Perhaps they were in dangerous dispute about territory or about a mate. They rose into the air again, fluttering close to each other, pecking at each other so that I couldn't tell if they were in combat or making love.

I was distracted from my bird-watching when I heard the post clatter through the hall letter-box and I left the breakfast room to collect it. At once I recognised the tiny handwriting on one of the brown envelopes. Mr or Mrs Anonymous again?

I opened it and read: 'Dr Simmonds is amongst the evil men of the world. All the knowledge Dr Simmonds has garnered from his medical textbooks is to no avail because those pages are only concerned with temporal being and such concerns do not embrace teachings offered from the Kingdom of God. Dr

Simmonds is wretched and does not know he is wretched. He is therefore false, a danger. He cometh with a lying smile, a stethoscope and a hypodermic syringe. Danger, danger. DANGER. Dr Simmonds deserves to be crushed.'

My correspondent obviously was off his or her head. I examined the parsimonious handwriting that sloped a little backwards. The paper itself had been extracted from some exercise book – a thin vertical red line made a margin on the left-hand side of the page which itself had grey horizontal lines across it. I screwed the paper up and threw it into the waste-paper basket.

Today, on my afternoon rounds, I noticed two graffiti in West Hampstead. An old one, KILROY WAS HERE, fading now; and another one, surely not there when I last came this way only days ago. At the traffic lights in West End Lane, bobby-soxers crowded the pavement outside the milk-bar; the other side of the road, a little further along, I could see on the iron parapet of the railway bridge someone had white-washed HISS IS INNOCENT.

How zealous graffiti-artists must be. Secretly they have to plan an expedition into the abandoned urban streets in the post-midnight hours, in order to bequeath us their urgent messages of anonymous protest or missionary belief. What insomniac satisfactions do they experience when, work accomplished, they return home with their paraphernalia – bucket of whitewash, big brush, torch?

Do such people feel a momentary thrill of power? The executioner is nameless and wears a mask. On the way home I imagined I might see writ large on a brick wall, DR SIMMONDS DESERVES TO BE CRUSHED.

March 4th

I attended the March meeting earlier this evening for two reasons. Firstly, because I hoped to see Yvonne Bloomberg there. (I admit it. Why shouldn't I admit it? I think of her more often than I should. There are occasions when I imagine I see her in the street but when I come close I am always mistaken.)

Secondly, because I have agreed to give my Broadhurst Gardens talk at the next meeting; and I wanted to have a better sense of the way things are handled there. Alas, Yvonne was not among the thirty-odd people present. I kept glancing at the door, hoping that she might be among the late-comers. I hardly heard the chairman – a permanent chairman, it would appear, Hugh Fisher – introducing the speaker, Anthony Crawford. 'Celebrated anthropologist... privileged he should visit our society... contributes regularly to the BBC's "Mind" programme... author of *Bushmen's Lore* ... etc. etc.'

He must have reached the halfway point of his lecture before he really conscripted my truant attention. Anthony Crawford related how natural observation informed Bushman tribal myths and their tribal legends. 'A lion,' he told us, 'coming across a herd of zebra or hartebeest will select one as his prey, one victim only. The others then know that they are safe and may even graze nearby. The lion is focused on one particular beast and will not be distracted from his intended quarry. Let me illustrate how such an observed phenomenon permeates one of the Bushmen's tales.'

I found the story he then unfolded, for some reason, haunting. It concerned a youthful hunter who, one hot afternoon, fell asleep, only to awake in the oven of a lion's mouth. The young man, realising his predicament, feigned to be dead. The lion, being thirsty, decided he needed to drink before devouring his meal. So, before visiting a nearby watering hole, the lion sequestered the young hunter between the stems of a zwart-storm tree. Painful twigs pierced the back of the young man's neck and brought tears to his eyes. This puzzled the lion who thought, 'Is this man dead?' The man remained motionless. The lion licked away the tears from the young man's eyes. 'Yes, the man is dead,' the lion thought and hurried away to the watering hole, intending to return soon enough to the zwart-storm tree. Meanwhile the hunter left the cage of the tree and ran zig-zag home to hide under a hartebeest skin, lest the lion would smell his footsteps and trace him to his village.

Sure enough, the lion came for his quarry. The villagers fired arrows at the thwarted creature. To no avail. The lion, unaffected, roared in anger. The villagers stabbed the lion with their assegai. To no avail. Had the animal been spellbound by a sorcerer? They offered a girl child to the lion. To no avail. The lion wanted only the young hunter whose tears it had drunk. It threatened to tear the villagers' huts asunder as it searched for the man that had been in its mouth.

The elders, frightened, delivered the hunter to the lion. 'And the lion bit the young man,' continued Anthony Crawford, 'bit the young man whose tears it had drunk. While the lion did so the villagers again shot arrows at it and stabbed it. And the lion spoke: this was the man it had been seeking, this was the one it would die for. And it died while the young man also lay dead.'

That Bushman story moved me. I thought of Michael Butler, he would like the story. He himself is a fine story-teller. Like the lion I had, as it were, drunk Michael's tears. And, like the lion, I would in due course kill him – not with devouring teeth but with merciful morphia.

After the meeting, when tea and biscuits were distributed, Hugh Fisher spoke to me. 'We'll have a larger audience than this for your lecture,' he assured me. 'People still refer to your Brains Trust contribution in January. Yvonne Bloomberg is one of your admirers. She says she finds your voice intriguing.' Fisher absurdly laughed, almost hooted. 'So do I,' he giggled.

Likes my voice! Maybe the man's queer. Before I could respond Mrs Levy joined us. 'That was a wonderful talk we heard, don't you think, doctor? Bushmen sound very interesting people but, to be honest, I wouldn't like one for a son-in-law.'

March 5th
'You should have come to the St David's Day thrash,' Rhys declared. 'Amy turned up on her own, got up like a Christmas decoration, all bounce and bosom. She asked after you.'

Rhys confided that afterwards he had taken her back to his place. He was waiting for me to ask him. I hesitated. I didn't want to seem to be kneeling before a keyhole. And yet I hoped he would elaborate. I was curious. Did he sleep with her? And did she remark on my deficiencies?

Only when he was leaving, putting on his overcoat in the hall, did he refer to Amy Middleton again. 'She's pregnant,' he said.

'What?'

'In the family way, a bun in the oven, a fatherless foetus.'

'How do you mean?'

'Well, I'm not the Daddy. Nor is Frank. She's up the creek without a paddle. I think she might want you to help her out. She said as much in a planned, impromptu aside. Take care, Robbie. The General Medical Council carry red-hot pokers and toasting forks.'

He was opening the front door. 'See you next week, kid.'

Outside, the noise of passing traffic, unusually loud for a Sunday evening. Then with the closing of the door the hall seemed peculiarly silent.

After Rhys had gone I picked up the *Doctor Glas* novel again for I only half recalled how he had dealt with a woman who had come to his surgery asking for her pregnancy to be terminated – against the Swedish law of 1905 as it continues to be now here: 'She could hardly speak for weeping. I replied as I always do. My usual high-minded peroration prepared for such occasions. Oath as a doctor! Duty! Respect for human life even the most frail! I recite by rote. Nor do I flinch in saying it all. So much suffering for so little pleasure...Respect for human life! Duty! Hypocritical? But an effective screen to hide behind and one which allows a doctor to avoid doing what should be done. Besides, why should I gamble my social position, my respectability, my future – everything, simply to help a stranger? And to rely on her discretion? That too, would be naive. Another woman, a friend in the same predicament, a word whispered to her of who can help and soon she and other pregnant ladies would be coming to my address in droves...'

Hear me, Dr Glas. I, Dr Simmonds, acknowledge such an affinity with you. I understand your loneliness, your non-physical attachment to a woman, a woman who is innocent – and your belief in purity of action, however risky.

I live here in 1950, you in a novel published in 1905. And yet you think my thoughts, speak words I could utter, accomplish deeds that I might yet emulate.

So Amy Middleton had conspired to entrap me; had invited me to a dinner party with no other guests, while her husband worked in Germany, so that she could sleep with me. Did she imagine that afterwards I would feel obligated? Over breakfast, perhaps, had she intended to confess to me that she was two months pregnant? No wonder she had not hinted at contraceptive imperatives. And I had been vain enough to think...

Let her come into my surgery. She will go away with no small change.

March 6th

I woke up this morning too early, into the darkness of 5 a.m. I don't know why my nubile Liverpool cousin, Marjorie, came to mind. The summer I had matriculated from the grammar school, I stayed with my aunt and uncle at a house they had rented in Hoylake. One of the bedrooms had been partitioned. I slept in one half, Marjorie in the other.

At eighteen, she was three years older than me and thought of me as a kid. We would go to the baths together – she was a fine swimmer. Beforehand, she would give me her full gorgeous attention and I would be her privileged confidant. As soon as we arrived she would ignore me. I didn't exist. Ashamed of me, I suppose, because of my acne and my fireworks scar. I watched young men older than Marjorie push her into the chlorine water and she would squeal and yet appear to be pleased. She was particularly petulant and yet at the same time, accommodating to one big, lascivious fellow called Paul. 'You're incorrigible,' she would say to him. 'You really are... incorrigible.' She liked the word 'incorrigible'.

At night I would wait for her to come to bed. I would stare that summer at the brown stain on the cracked ceiling. Pear-shaped, like Africa, it seemed as if it had been scorched by a man on stilts holding up a flat iron. After I heard her door close I would guess when she had put out the light. Then I would knock on the plywood partition. Three knocks. Soon her knocks came in reply. I doubt if she realised my knocks were my code for 'I... love... you.'

The house is not quite silent. (I'm writing this in my pyjamas. In an hour's time Edith will arrive to give me breakfast.) Genuine silence belongs only to such things as the stones and the clouds and their shadows. It is never completely at home within an inhabited building.

No person can feel lonely without being aware of other people.

March 10th, a.m., (before morning surgery)
I can't stick Anton Bloomberg. He chatters away ceaselessly when he rolls up his sleeve for his daily vitamin injection and takes his time before leaving my surgery. 'It would do you good,' he said to me yesterday like a schoolmaster, 'to listen to music every day, to make space for half an hour. I do. I know you recommend your patients to undertake physical exercise regularly. But music is equally necessary for our health. You know, when war broke out, I was initially interned at the Isle of Man as an enemy alien. Ridiculous. Fortunately a number of the

internees were musicians. Mozart saved my life. Yes, music is a holy anodyne, a spiritual unguent.'

Not only have I seen him briefly, or relatively briefly, at the surgery every day this week but also he buttonholed me while I was dining at the Cosmo on Wednesday evening. No Yvonne in sight, alas. Does she cook for herself alone?

It's not just the corporality of his physical appearance that irritates me – though with his thick lips and hooked nose he resembles a Nazi cartoon of a Jew to a T – it's everything. Even the way he eats makes me shudder. I know it's a trivial concern but I find it obnoxious the way he shovels food into the open gap of his mouth. He seems to swallow it all without chewing. And he holds his knife and fork without finesse.

Dr Glas, your Rev. Gregorius is a charmer compared with this fellow.

When I dared to ask after Yvonne he shifted his chair even closer to mine and leant towards me in that characteristic way of his, his face only inches away from mine and said softly, 'I've taken your advice, doctor. I'm playing it long. Besides, I've moved on. You know what I mean? As for Yvonne, she seems happy enough. While I listen to music she takes her exercise most mornings at the Finchley Road swimming baths.' He spoke of her with contempt.

This afternoon I visited the Butler household. I found Michael without disguise, looking so ill, so thin, like a concentration camp victim. I must have had Bloomberg's conversation in mind when I inappropriately suggested that, apart from the morphine injection, he might find listening to music consoling.

Somewhat aggressively Michael said, 'What do you suggest, doctor? Bach, Beethoven, or God Save the King?'

He relented and raised himself on his pillow to tell me one of his stories about Mongol soldiers deserting their posts on hearing Mongolian melodies.

'There you are,' I responded inadequately, 'the power of music.'

Michael laughed. 'It's just a story, a pretty story,' he said and laughed again without hilarity, disturbing me; a dying man's laugh.

Afterwards, alone with Rachel, I promised, 'It won't be long now. A matter of weeks probably. I shall come. Don't worry.'

'No,' she said. 'I've been talking to some friends who have been recommending Nightingale Manor. There's just a chance. You said yourself to me at the beginning – there's never such a thing as never in medicine.'

I had heard of Nightingale Manor. It had been run by a woman, Freda Dixon, whom some people thought of as a kind of saint, one who had famous healing powers. Her disciples still carried on her ministry though she had been dead some years now. It angered me that people in distress, knowing conventional medicine could do nothing for them, were taken for a financial ride by crazies or charlatans offering alternative medicine therapies.

'There's no point in spending money that way, Rachel,' I said. 'Leave things be.'

'It's not only the disciples of Freda Dixon offering treatment. They work along with doctors at that Institute. I've been told of a neighbour of ours who had a brain embolism, was unconscious, had been given up for lost and he has recovered.'

What could I say? Was it wrong for Rachel to hope for a miracle?

'I wonder,' she said, hesitating, 'I wonder, Dr Simmonds, whether you'd check the place out for me? I've phoned. I've made preliminary arrangements but I can cancel. I haven't told Michael yet.'

'You know I'm sceptical. I don't think you'd get the report you want from me.'

'I still would value your opinion.'

What was the point? I knew what my opinion would be. Visiting Nightingale Manor would not make me change my mind; but suddenly Rachel Butler, close to tears, grasped at my right hand, my deformed hand. 'Please,' she said, 'please.'

I could go tomorrow, I thought. A Saturday afternoon drive into the country would be no skin off my nose. It would not kill me to have a look at the place.

'There's a possibility I could go tomorrow afternoon,' I said. 'Where is Nightingale Manor exactly? Isn't it somewhere in Berkshire?'

It was terrible: Rachel Butler kissed my hand and cried as if I had given her back her husband's life. And there was, there is, no hope. No hope at all.

The Undertaker follows the Doctor like a shadow.

March 12th
Yesterday the March wind had become more benign as I drove through the Berkshire country lanes. Earlier, I had noticed how long catkins had been blown on the high branches of the Lombardy poplars either side of the road. And, as I drew closer to my destination, I thought how many others, from all over the world, had come this way towards Nightingale Manor because of the fame of Freda Dixon – all hoping for her healing touch in the same chapel and nursing home where the English 'saint' had no doubt walked one inch above the ground during the latter part of her life.

It is said that there have been cures of the incurable at Lourdes in France. They say cures have been effected by Padre Pio in Italy. There are many sophisticated and educated people who believe such cures to be attested and proven. Certainly there had been many credulous eminent churchmen who believed Freda Dixon to be another rare person who owned strange healing powers. The aristocracy had taken to her and not a few of them had bequeathed their riches to her ministry. I remember there was a celebrated Bishop who had had some association with Nightingale Manor and who had insisted that Freda Dixon had lived a life of devoted service and given herself without stint to the needy world of the sick. Well, perhaps. No doubt Freda Dixon did have a charismatic personality, a strong religious temperament which could convince patients or the relatives of patients that the sick could be brought back from death's portals. Mr Death, though, doubtless kept his gate wide open.

And there was another gate, the open large iron gate of Nightingale Manor, a stately mansion of England, transformed into a special kind of nursing home. At first, I could not see the building; the long, gravel drive twisted its way through extensive woodland. I observed the yellow-green flowers of dog's mercury abundantly present on the ground below the trees. The wood was bird-haunted.

The narrow gravel road rose over a small hill and at once I could see before me the mansion itself and its adjoining private chapel. A great bell was clanging and some minutes later, when I had parked the car, the sun came out from behind a cloud to pick out, like an unkind stage spotlight, the faces of the weary and the sick who were filing into the church.

When I joined the procession and walked into the beautiful, ornate church a woman smiled and said gently to me, as if I were myself one of the patients, 'The day of our death is the most beautiful of our life.' Before I could reply to that shameful humbug the service began. I became aware of stained glass windows, blue carpet and blue ceiling, Mary's colour. The sun came and went, drizzling briefly through the stained glass on to the gold-glittering candelabras and the golden statuettes of angels. Everywhere blue, the colour of healing; and gold, the colour of money. My old friend, Charlie Forster could have a thriving connection with a place like this . . .

Soon I observed a priest, (I later discovered him to be the Reverend Douglas Clifton, no doubt a priest as egregious as the

Reverend Gregorius) laying hands on those who inched forwards. A young father hugged in his arms a child of about three years old. The boy's small hand kept twitching curiously, bent on the wrist in an odd posture. The little boy, I could see, was a spastic.

The Rev. Clifton placed his hands firmly on the head of the child and prayed as did others in the pews. Afterwards, the service over, I guessed the father of the spastic child would donate a hefty thanks offering. When he started to write the cheque God would let him know that he should give more.

An hour later, I sat with the Reverend Clifton, who had shed his cassock, inside the elegantly furnished, delightful, airy drawing room of the Nightingale mansion. I couldn't help glancing at his well-manicured hands which, only an hour earlier, had touched uselessly the head of the spastic child. Behind him, on the piano, I could see a photograph of Freda Dixon, wearing a hat and a coat with a fur collar.

'Speak to Dr Yates who practises in the village,' he urged me. 'He comes to our services. He will testify that in the chapel there have been wonderful cures of hopeless cases. We'd be glad to receive any of your patients, doctor.'

'You know, Father,' I said, looking around the luxurious room, 'I associate holiness with poverty. Freda Dixon wasn't exactly poor.'

Through the window I could see the rolling green grounds of Nightingale Manor sweeping down to a lake and then onwards to the far woods.

'If Freda had had her way she would have taken a vow of poverty,' the priest said. 'Her only real extravagance was that fine piano behind me.'

'Did she play well?'

'As a matter of fact she did.'

'Ah yes,' I said, 'music is a holy anodyne, a spiritual unguent.'

'Exactly.'

The Rev. Clifton hesitated. 'I know some people think she was

92

a charlatan. What evidence have they for saying so?'

'Why do you think they should make such an accusation?' I countered.

'Because of the money, I suppose. There have been others who have claimed to heal people by the laying on of hands, but they have not had God's gift.'

I learnt that there were dozens of people, disciples all of them, working at Nightingale Manor, trying to carry on where Freda Dixon left off – all these were women who having been 'cured' by the 'saint' in turn wished to help heal others.

'And, of course, there's myself and the Medical Director, Dr Thomas Brook, who as you know is held in high esteem by the medical profession generally and, of course, is adored by all here. I'm so sorry he's not here to greet you.'

'Is he playing golf this afternoon?' I asked.

The priest pretended not to hear my snide remark but waxed on about how faith can restore integrated happiness in sick people until he became intoxicated with righteousness.

When I left the manor and strolled over to my Morris Minor dozens of rooks flew blackly over my head and circled around the church uttering their hoarse, admonitory cries. I drove away, down the narrow gravel road, and then over to the other side of the hill until I could no longer see the manor nor the church in the side mirror. It had been a wasted journey. The Rev. Clifton had spoken as if God was in the telephone directory and that he was conversant with the number. He had not heard that Nietzsche had pronounced God to be dead, that earlier Darwin had buried Him, and Marx had written His obituary. I know, though, that whatever scornful confection I reported to Rachel Butler, her husband, Michael, would be dispatched to the Freda Dixon Institute at Nightingale Manor.

I'm writing this late at night and I'm still upset because of my row with Rhys. Before I could bring out the chessboard he complained, 'I didn't sleep last night. It continued to be 3 a.m. for four hours with an outside door banging in the wind. But it was Amy who kept me awake.'

'You were with Amy Middleton?'

'No, no. I was worrying about her. She might go under, Robbie, go down to where they don't play billiards.'

'What?'

'One minute she's as high as benzedrine. She's standing on stilts on the top of Snowdon, wild-eyed like Bette Davis. The next, she's down there where it's don't forget the diver, Robbie.'

'Well, it's not your problem, Rhys.'

Then Rhys told me how Amy's husband had, during an interrogation, frisked one particular high Nazi of a lethal suicide phial. 'The sort Goering took to say Ta Ta to the world,' continued Rhys. 'The point is the idiot brought that phial home. It's in a drawer somewhere in that house in Richmond.'

'Did Amy Middleton tell you that?'

'Yes.'

'It's bluff,' I said.

'It's a cry for help,' argued Rhys. 'And a threat. She could cross the Lethe, Robbie. I said I'd ask you. And I'm asking you, pal.'

I didn't want anything to do with her under any circumstances. She had tried to entrap me into a sexual spider's web and had failed. I had slept with her. So what? As some poet once wrote: 'Let me make it plain:/I find this frenzy insufficient reason/For conversation when we meet again.' Only I didn't want to meet her again.

'You could go and see her. Calm her down. Persuade her, at least, to hand that phial over to you.'

'I'm not getting involved.'

'You can't be struck off the Register by simply talking to the lady,' said Rhys, raising his voice. 'Supposing she takes that stuff. What is it? Cyanide?'

I know very little about Hydrogen cyanide (prussic acid), except that it is a colourless liquid, intensely poisonous. Probably the fatal dose for a man is only one-twentieth of a gram. Dr Glas used it. He was certain that when he poisoned the Rev. Gregorius his victim would succumb within seconds and there would be no overt signs of asphyxia.

I tried to change the subject. Every year, on our respective birthdays, Rhys and I go to the theatre together and dine well afterwards. I will be forty next Friday, on March 17th, and I had already booked two stall tickets to see a Pirandello play, *As You Desire Me*, which has just opened at the Embassy Theatre.

'It's with Mary Morris,' I told Rhys. 'I've ... '

'Stop nattering on about the theatre,' he interrupted me. 'Come out of your bird-cage, mun. Show some pity for the woman. When I left her she was as white as shaving lather. How often have I asked you for favours? Never. NEVER. Stop squinting at me like that.'

'I'm sorry,' I said. 'There's such a thing as a medical ethical code if you are ... '

'You're heartless. Especially when it comes to women, you're heartless. And a prude. Smug with it.'

I boiled at that. I suppose I shouldn't have gone off steaming but what right had Rhys to speak to me like that? I said more than I meant to – I referred to Rhys's own character – how he was in the real sense a play-boy, one who never did any real work. And as for Amy fucking Middleton she was not only dangerous as far as I was concerned, but she was a slut. 'She's anybody's,' I concluded. 'I despise her.'

Rhys became ominously quiet. I could hear the clock ticking on the mantelpiece. He took a cigarette out of its packet and then put it back again. He rose from the chair. 'By the way,' he said, 'I'm playing in a tournament next Friday night. At Prompt Corner. I forgot it was your birthday.'

'No problem,' I said, trying not to reveal how disarrayed I felt.

'I'd better go,' Rhys said. 'I'm too hung over to play chess. I need to have a kip.'

And all I said was, 'Of course,' before seeing him silently to the front door.

March 14th
As soon as the last patient hobbled out of my surgery this morning (he had a sprained ankle) I let Edith know that I intended to go for a swim. She rose from her usual chair near the kitchen stove and, incredulously, peered out of the half-steamed-up windows.

'It's raining,' she said blankly.

Indeed it was. The drainpipe on the side wall of the house next door needed fixing. Gushes of water spouted out of a joint to slap the soaked concrete path below. And thin rivulets of rain tracked down the windows of our own kitchen.

'I'm not going to swim in the gutters. I'm going to the Finchley Road Baths,' I said.

'In the Finchley Road Baths?' repeated Edith.

'I need the exercise.'

'Are you sure? I heard you coughing a lot this morning.'

The familiar way Edith fusses over me and bosses me around you would think she was a doting aunt, the sort who orders you to put your gloves on when you go out.

I hoped I might find Yvonne at the baths. It did not augur well. It was already late in the morning. She was unlikely to linger there past midday. All the way to the swimming baths I recalled how my father initially tried to teach me how to swim. My Liverpool cousin, Marjorie, had been staying with us at the time and I had felt ashamed when my father and mother had crossed verbal swords in front of her. (My cousin was already to me a young woman, thirteen years of age with real breasts.) I remember I had been wheedling my mother, telling her how Ron, the boy next door, had been given a new bike by his parents.

'Most of my gang have one,' I said. 'Terry's got a Raleigh, John's got a Rudge and David's got a Sunbeam.'

My mother, ironing, had probably only been half listening but she said, 'All right, maybe next Christmas, we'll see.'

'I'm here too,' my father suddenly complained. 'I live in this house too, you know.'

'Sometimes,' my mother pronounced.

'That boy always addresses you,' my father argued. 'It's as if I'm not in the same room. He never even looks me in the eye.'

'Don't be silly,' my mother said.

My father confronted me, 'You've got a mother who gives you anything you ask for.'

My mother flared. 'And you're not a better father than you are a husband.'

She then relentlessly intoned a litany of misdeeds until my father abruptly walked out of the room. I witnessed Marjorie listening to all this, big-eyed. Later that same morning, as if to make recompense, my father offered to take us both to the local Baths and teach me how to swim. 'Marjorie's a champion swimmer,' I said. 'She can do the crawl, the breast stroke and the butterfly. She'll show me.' I saw the muscle in my father's cheek contract.

His idea of instructing me how to swim was to put one large hand under my belly and persuade me to bring both my feet off the unstable, zig-zag floor of the pool. Somehow my feet would not obey messages from my head and my father began to lose patience. It was some time before I could manage to obey his increasingly titanic commands. At last I managed it. There I was, triumphantly kicking the water with both my feet when he treacherously took his hand away and I sank, to come up gasping and choking, my eyes stinging with chlorine. I heard my father laughing. That was the worst of it. Soon I could speak and I shouted, 'You big bloody bully.' And he only laughed again.

I didn't mind at all that he then gave up on me and joined some other adults near the changing cubicles. I stood miserably shivering at the shallow end while Marjorie, indifferent and full of zest, all crawl and breast stroke, swam innumerable lengths, up and down, up and down.

At Finchley Road Baths no Yvonne was in sight. Before changing into my bathing trunks, I listened to the blank explosions of those diving from the spring-board at the deep end and I remembered what a defeated small boy I had once been.

I phoned Rachel Butler and she told me how willingly Michael had agreed to be installed at Nightingale Manor. Maybe I have been too harsh. Religion may help him as it has others. The torture of chronic pain, with exquisite economy, prompts a man to cry out to God. They will extract a pretty penny, though, from the Butlers in exchange for their crumbs of comfort.

I think Rachel Butler, unresigned, is seeking more than such crumbs. She hopes for a blazing miracle. Undeniably, some fringe-healers, confident of their own healing powers, have had a quota of successes when treating patients with stress-related disorders. The emotionally disturbed patient is more likely to respond to and have faith in an optimistic healer with impervious confidence in their own power than the average doctor who, like myself, generally is beset with any number of scientific doubts and reservations. But medicasters, even those as charismatic as Freda Dixon, must perforce be defeated when treating a terminal organic condition such as that which afflicts Michael Butler.

I envy true charismatics only in that they have some strangeness about them, something that does not permit too much familiarity, something akin to distance, something of fearful mountains unclimbed. When your nearness is far, suggested the poet Rainer Maria Rilke, then your distance is like the very stars.

By talking to myself, I hear what I am thinking.

March 16th

Anton Bloomberg almost waltzed into my consulting room for his final Vitamin B appointment. He carried a parcel, a gift for me – a record. He invaded my breathing space as usual even as

I undid the fancy paper wrapping and read the print on the record's cover: *Artur Schnabel spielt Franz Schubert.*

'Schubert,' I said. 'Thank you.'

'A composer who can evoke a mood with just a few economical notes,' lectured Bloomberg.

'You shouldn't have done. It wasn't necessary.'

'You've done me good,' insisted my fleshy patient. 'I've stopped wheezing at night. It's either the Vitamin B or the fact that, presently, I'm more sexually satisfied.'

I said nothing as I prepared to give him the injection. He rolled up his sleeve and I noticed for the first time that Edith had put fresh daffodils in the corner vase. What did he mean – 'more sexually satisfied'? Did this remark, coupled with his evident buoyancy, signify that Yvonne had opened herself voluntarily to him? Was she now tarnished, without spiritual virginity?

'And Yvonne is content?' I asked.

'You, doctor, should get yourself a woman. It would do you good.'

He didn't realise he was being impudent. As he rolled down the sleeve of his shirt and reached for his jacket he sounded off about music again, about how, as a boy in Hamburg, he had loved going with his sister to the opera. 'But when I returned from the Isle of Man I discovered that the Covent Garden Opera House here had been transformed into a dance hall for the duration of the war.'

I don't know what made me say that, like Hitler, I admired Wagner, that Wagner was a great man, not only as a musician, but a prophetic figure. I heard the ambiguity in my own voice and Anton Bloomberg must have divined it also for he suddenly accused me, 'You don't like Jews, do you, doctor? Like Wagner, you are anti-semitic.'

Outraged, I stuttered. And he, contrite, added, 'I mean you are so conscious of Jews being Jews.'

I suppose I am conscious of the Jewishness of some of my patients and acquaintances – how could it be otherwise with Anton Bloomberg's Jew-face?

'I mean you say things that are offensive to Jews though you don't seem to be aware you are doing so.'

'I don't need a sermon from you,' I said vehemently.

He put out his hand, his podgy hand. I dislike shaking hands with people. I sheer away from unnecessary contact because of my own hand. I could not refuse this gesture of his though. I forced myself to smile and shake hands with him. Soon I was seeing him out of my surgery and, oblivious of my feelings, he left as cheerily as he came in.

Jews! Doubtless, when a small child, I picked up unconsciously all kinds of prejudices. My mother would make derogatory remarks about Jews though her attitude, I feel sure, was rooted in class-prejudice rather than in real anti-semitism. She had all kinds of frivolous prejudices – against homosexuals and those with the wrong colour skin. I remember how she warned me, albeit laughingly, when I was a small boy to take great care to avoid stepping on the black joins in the pavement stones, 'Else, when you grow up, Robbie, you'll marry a black lady!'

Worse, when it came to anti-semitism, was the overt hostility of my Sunday-school teacher to 'Israelites' as he called them, and what they had done to our Lord. I recall admiring the black shirt he often wore. Did he leave his receipt with me? How many people, I wonder, can choose to over-ride stencilled-in prejudices. I think I can.

Mrs Audrey Townsend was a relatively new patient. Since her menopause she had been suffering from migrainous headaches.

'When my husband brings back business associates to the house,' she related, 'I'm required to entertain them. Alas, as soon as the front door bell rings I know I'm in for it. A zig-zag line of light interposes itself between my eyes and any object I look at. And I feel sick. I have to ... '

At this point the telephone clamoured for attention. She stopped speaking and put her hands over her ears as if the sound of the telephone was intolerable. Generally, Edith accepts the telephone calls during my morning consultations but it seemed that on this occasion she was in the loo or something.

'Excuse me,' I said to Mrs Townsend as I picked up the persistent phone on my desk. It turned out to be Charlie Forster. He wanted me to have dinner with him.

'This evening?'

'Sorry about the short notice,' he apologised. 'My turn to take you out. Meet me at the Plurabelle at 8 p.m. OK? I'll book.'

We exchanged other quotidian pleasantries and I must admit our dialogue was a little prolonged – though not so extended as to warrant Mrs Townsend's hostile reaction. I put the phone down, thinking that the Plurabelle was the most expensive of restaurants, but when I looked up I met Mrs Townsend's steady, discontented eyes. She had obviously heard everything I had said to Charlie and she bridled, all porcupine needles, all wasp stings.

'Couldn't that social phone call have waited?' she scolded me. 'Couldn't you have said you were with a patient? Have you no consideration for those who sit anxiously in this chair?'

Doctors do not invariably command the respect of patients these days. Some doctors have reported how they have been assaulted in their consulting rooms. Possibly a few have been too blunt in articulating this or that diagnosis or prognosis, having forgotten that without hope the heart may break. A number of patients may have become violent because they sensed that these tactless truth-tellers were gaining some sadistic pleasure in imparting bad news. There are patients, undeniably, who would behead the messenger however gently tentative the physician may be in ventilating a diagnosis – especially if that messenger is transparently full of gusto and brimming with physical health! Perhaps that is why Plato believed that doctors should not be robust in health 'and should have all manners of disease in their own persons.'

Mrs Townsend staggered me. 'You wouldn't treat me like that if I were a man,' she accused me unjustifiably.

'I only stopped a moment to take a phone call,' I protested.

'Now, please, calm down, Mrs Townsend.'

'You weren't listening to me when I was complaining about...'

'I certainly was. You were telling me about your visual aura that preceded a migrainous attack when you had to entertain guests.'

'You don't know how excruciating a migraine attack can be,' she said. She stood up. 'You're cold,' she continued. 'You've got ice where your soul should be.'

Audrey Townsend is an over-sensitive, tense individual and perhaps I should have been more careful about Charlie's telephone call. I did my best to humour her. I think to no avail. She will probably seek out another doctor to treat her migraine.

It had not been a good morning. I'd also managed to provoke Anton Bloomberg.

I do not think I have ice in my soul.

Charlie Forster had evidently triumphed formidably at a recent poker game. After we had settled comfortably into our chairs and the volatile, too attentive waiter had poured out the wine and ceased to flit around the table like a mad bat, Charlie produced a small brown parcel and an envelope from his briefcase. The envelope contained a cheque.

'I remembered it's your birthday tomorrow so I thought it would be a good time to repay my debt and also give you this token birthday present.'

'Thanks very much.' I don't know why I felt so grateful for receiving my own money back!

'No doubt you've got things lined up for tomorrow?'

I could feel myself reddening. I wondered whether I should ask him if he'd like to take up Rhys's spurned ticket for the Embassy Theatre.

'I hope you'll like the book,' Charlie grinned. 'I've wrapped it up in brown paper because it's pornography. I was in the USA recently. I've brought it through Customs unscathed.'

He was joking. At least, I guessed he was joking. I started to unwrap his tantalising present.

'No, no,' he said, 'Leave it till tomorrow and think of me on your birthday.' Then he added, lifting his glass, 'Drink up, Robbie. This isn't Algerian plonk.'

I did not invite Charlie to join me at the Pirandello play. He had a wife to consider and I had only one spare ticket. Besides, I decided by the time the main course arrived that I should distance myself from my old friend. He was no longer the Charlie Forster I had known as a student. I disliked the way he rhapsodised about his group practice where, apart from the link-up with the osteopath, Tom Taylor, he and his partner, the hypnotist, Tony Dickinson, had been joined now by another Westminster alumnus, Freddie Hill, a most unsavoury character.

While I was doing my medical student stint on the midwifery and gynaecology firm, he had been the Junior Registrar. Because of a hushed-up gynaecological 'accident' Freddie Hill left Westminster and, avoiding metropolitan obloquy, had migrated to an unlikely patch in the West Country where he had put up his brass plate as a General Practitioner.

Some years later, before the war, I read a newspaper report about a certain Dr F. Hill, a Somerset GP who could foretell what sex an unborn baby would be. As a result of that newspaper report (under the headline CLAIRVOYANT DOCTOR) his burgeoning reputation for accurate predictions spread and pregnant women flocked to his care. His practice richly thrived.

I can't remember who told me – maybe it was Charlie – the secret of his 'clairvoyancy'. He would inform Mrs Smith that she was going to have a girl. 'I'll enter my prediction here in this ledger,' he would tell the patient. Then opposite Mrs Smith, he wrote 'boy'. If Mrs Smith gave birth to a girl doubtless she would tell all her friends and neighbours about the clever Dr Hill. If, on the other hand, she had a boy and challenged Freddie Hill, he would solemnly produce his ledger, turn to the appropriate page and say, 'No you're mistaken, Mrs Smith. As you can see here I predicted you would have a boy.'

'Freddie Hill?' I said.

'Yes,' said Charlie, 'he knows his stuff.'

Charlie handed me his card with its three names, Dr Charles Forster, Dr Anthony Dickinson and Dr Frederick Hill, printed above a Harley Street address.

'So, if you have some rich patients dissatisfied with National Health offerings, think of us. You must have some filthy rich old patients who need to be rejuvenated.'

'Like me you mean?'

'I'm treating quite a few old men with a refinement of the Steinach method.'

'What about the old women?' I commented sourly.

'C'mon, Robbie, we've known for a hundred years that tying off the sperm ducts causes more blood to flow into the testicles. You remember Professor Stanton told us about Steinach and the rats when we were doing Physiology together?'

I did remember. Steinach tied off one sperm duct in each male senile rat, leaving the duct of the other testicle alone so that, if rejuvenation took place, the rat would still be able to breed. Prior to the operation, the old rats showed the usual outward signs and symptoms of senility. They lay about listlessly, their eyes dull; they no longer cleaned themselves and their skin showed bald patches. They even ignored their favourite pieces of fat bacon when these were offered to them on a stick. Their sex instinct, too, had completely vanished. They had no interest in female rats and they retreated from young male rats, showing none of the pugnaciousness they would have displayed if they had not been senile.

I recalled Professor Stanton's enthusiastic voice, his eyes bright, as he told us students the results of Steinach's operation. 'New hair grew on their skins and the bald patches vanished. They became agile, ate with relish, fought young rats, and experienced a sexual paroxysm.' The professor's voice diminished to a confidential whisper. 'The once senile rats exhibited insatiable desire for the females. Alarming sexual potency! Not only were these hitherto senile rats youthful again – their life span increased also.' I believe Stanton would have tried to rejuvenate himself eventually but he had a fatal heart attack too early, long before he experienced the ravages of age.

'I've been looking into these experiments,' Charlie continued. 'The rejuvenation effect lasted months – that's a long time for a rat. The Leydig interstitial cells of the testicle were responsible for it all. Microscopic examination of sections from the testicle revealed these cells had grown larger and had increased in size.'

'So you're carrying out Steinach's operation on human beings?' I asked.

'Yep. It's simple. Refinements of it. Listen, I've had one old fella, well into his seventies – an ex-banker actually – with marked arteriosclerosis and his sexual desire has returned after an absence of a decade and happily he has also the ability to take advantage of it.'

I glanced around the tables of the Plurabelle. Many of the diners looked old and in need of rejuvenation. Everyone was so well dressed. The place was so expensive they were all probably eating their supertax expenses. Suddenly I felt a spurt of hate towards the place and all those dining there – even the waiters, especially ours who hovered obsequiously nearby.

'There are some dangers in the Steinach op,' I said. 'What if...'

Charlie interrupted me. 'You're so frightened of taking risks, Robbie. You always have stuck to the narrow path, frightened of exploring the wild dark wooded pastures on either side. Ever since I've known you, you've avoided taking chances.'

'I took a chance,' I defended myself, 'when I lent you a thousand pounds!'

'And you don't trust people either,' he said, ignoring my remark. 'I think it's because of your boyhood fireworks accident.'

In turn I ignored that. I thought instead how in medical history so often doctors and quacks who have produced rejuvenation treatments have equated longevity with sexuality. The physicians of King David's era tried to revitalise the old dying king by commanding Abishag, the most beautiful young virgin of all Israel, to share his bed. 'And the damsel was very fair, and cherished the king and ministered to him: but the king knew her not.' Then there was that famous Dutch physician Hermann Boerhaave who, in the 18th century, recommended a deviation of the Abishag therapy. He placed two healthy naked youths, one on either side of an ailing burgomaster – with what results no one knows.

As we were leaving the opulent Plurabelle, Charlie said, 'Put some money on Freebooter for the Grand National.'

'Freebooter?'

'That's a red-hot tip, honest.'

As we strolled on we could hear some busker playing an accordion. I could not resist remarking, 'Your clairvoyant partner, Freddie Hill, predicts it, I suppose.'

Charlie just shook his head sadly. 'Just the same old Robbie Simmonds. The same upright, costive character. Don't let the world get you down again, love. If you don't back horses, try the Stock Exchange.'

'A Jewish Monte Carlo,' I said.

Passing the busker, Charlie dropped more coins than was necessary into the forlorn cap on the pavement and I thought how he had also over-tipped the too attentive waiter at the Plurabelle. One of these days Charlie will be coming back to me to borrow more cash! The accordion player's familiar tune faded yet stayed as we ambled on:

> In Scarlet town, where I was born
> There was a fair maid dwellin'
> Made every lad cry Well-a-day!
> Her name was Barbara Allen.
> All in the merry month of May
> When green buds they were swellin'
> Young Jimmy Grove on his death-bed lay,
> For love of Barbara Allen...

Back home I undid the brown parcel. Why wait until birthday time? I felt the back of my neck go cold as I read the title of the book: *Dr Glas*, a novel by Hjalmar Söderberg. It was uncanny that Charlie Forster had, of all possible books, given me this American translation of the Swedish novel which so often, lately, had occupied and haunted my thoughts. Uncanny? I suppose we use that word when we can provide no plausible, mechanistic, satisfying explanation for some strange incident or significant coincidence. I know the very word 'uncanny' has a secondary meaning in some languages: daemonic.

Ever since I returned from my dinner date with Charlie, for hours now, I've been writing these entries in my journal. It's long past midnight. So it's my birthday already. March 17th. I am forty years of age. Time passes. The flowers are dying in the funeral parlour.

Sometimes, very late as now, when I'm very tired, I experience an uneasy, indefinable, ridiculous feeling that a spirit is endeavouring to possess me! But now I wonder whether Dr Glas truly existed outside the pages of Söderberg's novel – that his books were more a biography than fiction.

March 18th
I did not see the Pirandello play and dine on my own afterwards. Soon after I arrived at the Embassy Theatre, I stood in the foyer and suddenly observed, among the audience flocking in, Anton Bloomberg, holding open the door solicitously for a young woman accompanying him. She unwound a silky, green, diaphanous scarf from about her head and shook her night-black hair loose. Who was this woman? 'I'm more sexually satisfied,' Bloomberg had said to me in my surgery. I had a vague sense of a door opening somewhere else. The woman with Bloomberg

smiled up at him, her slash of red lipstick too ostentatious. Her inviting smile was not filial. She reminded me of a gypsy.

While Bloomberg had his back to me I quit the foyer, having quickly decided I would prefer to be with Yvonne than see the play. For a couple of hours, at least, her husband would be at the Embassy Theatre. It would be my birthday treat – just to be with Yvonne.

I hurried to my parked car in Eton Avenue and I understood the cliché 'light of heart' as I drove through the lamplight and shadows of the suburban streets towards the block of modern luxury flats close to the bombed derelict house. At its portentous entrance I would press the bell, and soon afterwards I would be rising in the lift to the 4th floor where Yvonne would be waiting for me, as in a legend, surprised at my appearance, but welcoming me like a long-lost brother coming home to his sister. Inside the apartment she would be about to have her evening meal and, of course, would invite me to dine with her in easy companionship. 'I mustn't stay,' I would say. 'I was seeing a patient nearby so I thought I'd call to see how you are both getting on.' She would insist that I should break bread with her and raise a glass of good red wine on this night of my fortieth birthday. She would be my friend, my collaborator, my ally. The time would be Soon and the apartment would be our Stage.

Alas, before I could get out of the car I spotted her walking from the block of flats towards me. I realised my reverie had been juvenile, frivolous. I waited until she was almost alongside my Morris Minor before I opened the car door and called out, 'Yvonne.'

She seemed delighted to see me. 'I'm just on my way to a Broadhurst Gardens committee meeting,' she explained. 'We have to arrange our programme for the summer season. We're all so looking forward to your talk in April.'

Yvonne did not query why I was sitting in a parked car in the darkness, close to her home. I had no need to tell lies about a patient I had visited in the vicinity. Perhaps she had guessed and delicately resolved not to probe.

'I'll drive you over to Broadhurst Gardens,' I said adamantly. 'I'm going that way.'

She sat in the passenger seat next to me and when I reached for the gears I accidentally touched her thigh. She never said a word. And I never said a word all the way to Broadhurst Gardens. The silence in the car did not discomfort me nor do I think it was burdensome to her. It was a contented silence that did not even father thoughts. I was confident that she not only recognised my affection for her but also reciprocated that pure affection – though, being married, her gestures must necessarily be muted. I think we understood each other without the approximation of words, intuitively.

Only when I had parked the car behind John Barnes and she had half opened the door, did she say softly, 'I'm so grateful to you, Robbie. That course of bromides you have given my husband has worked wonderfully. You told Anton it would subdue his libidinous needs and you were right. Thankfully, he doesn't try to touch me now. Strange, it makes me respect him more.'

Because she kept the door of the Morris Minor slightly ajar the small light on the roof had come on and, again, I felt almost breathless seeing Yvonne's truly beautiful face so clearly.

'Where is Anton tonight?' I asked.

'Poor dear,' she replied. 'All the week he's been working late at the office. The auditors are due.'

She bent forward and kissed me gently on the cheek. I breathed in her perfume. Then she almost ran away from the car having slammed fast the passenger door so that the little roof light went out. I sat there behind the steering wheel, feeling bruised in the dark and thinking, Bloomberg – what a wanton bastard! Bromides indeed!

I drove as fast as I could back down the Finchley Road, past Swiss Cottage, down Avenue Road into Regent's Park. I was heading for the desperate bright lights of Soho where I would have a solitary dinner in one of the restaurants. As I drove I thought how, after the performance at the Embassy, Bloomberg would accompany his seductive gypsy back to her place. Presumably she would invite him in and sooner rather than later they would, unclothed, be clasping each other like the slimy frogs in the ponds of the Heath.

I parked the car outside the railings of Soho Square. Somewhere within that patch of green stood the stony statue of Charles II who, with his back to the stews of Soho, stared blindly up at the obscure stars. I walked into Greek Street past the House of Charity, a sanctuary for destitute women. Almost at once prostitutes emerged from cave-like doorways and from the seedy dark alleyways to whisper promises of illicit ecstasies. So many of them. The area needs cleaning up. Gladstone used to come this way, night after night, intent on rescuing two or three of these 'fallen ones'. He would take them home to the care of his wife. As an MP at that time declared, Gladstone managed 'to combine his missionary meddling with a keen appreciation of a pretty face'. What would he have thought of that neon-lit advertisement, GIRLS, GIRLS, GIRLS or the dingy sauna and so-called massage parlour across the road?

Outside the Nell Gwynne Al-Nite Club, I was examined threateningly by a man with a Maltese face wearing a Humphrey Bogart trilby. Edward Burra painted men like this. Before I reached L'Escargot Bienvenue restaurant I was solicited by a particularly young prostitute standing in a doorway. In the inefficient lamplight she reminded me of that angel-like schoolgirl who, in 1946, had attempted to drag me into the nocturnal wild garden of an empty house.

'Come in for a drink, sir,' the young prostitute suggested softly. I smiled, walked on. I didn't go into L'Escargot. Though it was nearly nine o'clock I didn't feel hungry. Instead, I went into a pub and ordered a double whisky in celebration of my birthday. Two men at the bar talked loud enough for me to hear their idiosyncratic dialogue:

'An' I don't like pelmets.'

'They're nice with curtains.'

'Pelmets? I can't abide them.'

'I don't see why you should feel so passionately about pelmets.'

'I *hate* 'em.'

The pub had a fused look. It was about as cheerful as a mortuary so after my celebration drink with which I said to myself, 'Happy birthday, Robbie,' I left the pub and retraced my steps, feeling at a loss, wondering whether I should just claim my car and drive straight home. Or if I should swallow my pride and visit the Prompt Corner at South End Green where Rhys would be playing his tournament chess game.

Again I was approached by the same young prostitute in the doorway who, like a mantra, uttered, 'Come in for a drink, sir.' And I wondered how come one so young, a mere schoolgirl, should be on the game? Stupidly, I stopped and said, 'All right . . . But just for a drink.' In the lit, dilapidated hallway I read the notice: MODEL. Suzette. 2nd Floor. Suzette, if it was Suzette, led me up the uncarpeted staircase that creaked underfoot and I could see how unattractively thin her bare legs were. At one point she turned to ensure that I was following her. She did not resemble in any way the angel-like schoolgirl of Netherhall Gardens. This young girl had an unlined doll's face with dyed flaxen hair and somewhat protruding blue eyes.

A door on the landing of the second floor opened to a room even more cheerless than the pub I had recently quit. At least it had a lit gas fire close to which sat an ageing stout person of indeterminate sex wearing slacks.

'He wants a drink, Fifi.'

'Only a drink?'

'Only a drink,' I said firmly.

There was a bar, or rather a counter, behind which a couple of shelves were decorated with a variety of empty wine and liqueur bottles. More worrying, a toxic lime-green curtain bisected the room. What was behind it? Maybe it simply concealed a bed but I had heard tales of people being robbed in Soho in places such as this.

A small table with two chairs had been placed to one side of the puttering gas fire. The girl sat down in one chair, her skirt inordinately high. Nude thighs. Thin legs. A 'golden' chain about one ankle. She indicated I should sit in the other chair. What am I doing here? I thought. I'd have one quick drink, then go. The room smelt of poverty.

'How did you get that 'orrible scar on your face?' the girl asked.

'What's your name?' I queried. 'Is it Suzette?'

'You can call me Bunny,' she said with a simian smile.

'Bunny?'

'Yes. What's your name, pet?'

'My name?'

'Yeh.'

'Dr Glas,' I said involuntarily, surprising myself.

Bunny laughed. 'Dr Glass. Oh, I can see right through you all right.'

The ageing woman, for woman she must have been since she was called Fifi, stood before us holding two glasses. 'Gin OK, darling?' She put both glasses on the white linoleum-covered table without waiting for an answer.

'Ten shillings,' said the gravel-voiced, masculine Madame Fifi. Ten shillings! Ridiculously steep, but I had no wish to haggle.

I fished out the note from my wallet. As I was doing so, Bunny immediately picked up her glass like a veteran and emptied it. 'Probably tap-water,' I thought but when I sipped at the clear fluid in my glass it definitely had a trace of gin in it. Before I could return the glass to the table top Bunny outrageously placed her small hand on my trouser zip. 'Oh,' she said, 'You're a big boy. Shall we? Five quid.'

I brushed her hand away. 'Two quid,' Fifi demanded, putting out her hand. 'You can't have her on appro.'

I stood up. 'Sorry,' I said and made for the door. I felt so inadequate, so stupid. I glanced back and saw, as in an immobile photograph, their two rejected sullen faces staring at me.

I rushed down the clattering staircase. Outside, anonymous in Greek Street, I felt liberated and I walked swiftly to Soho Square to the enclosed safety of my car. I drove home where I made myself some toast and cheese before going to bed.

I read a little while before switching off the light. When I closed my eyes I conjured up the face of Yvonne and touched myself. So endeth my birthday.

March 19th
This Sunday afternoon is hollow. No Rhys, no chess. I should go out and walk on the Heath, smell the fresh air, cleanse myself from Friday night's misadventures, feel the good earth underfoot. Outside the small birds are fluting threnodies from the high tree-tops in their springtime sexual agony.

I did not go out – instead read the *Observer* and *The Sunday Times*, perused the book reviews of books I shall never read, film notices of films I'll never see. When I turned to the main news of statesmen by murder fed and by murder clothed, an aeroplane happened to throb over ominously, provoking thoughts of a nuclear holocaust. Soon after, another plane flew by so low I went to the garden door and looked out.

The blundering noise of the plane, which I could not see, faded. But as I stood there, a rainbow visited the sky, became more and more visible, and I thought of my Sunday School teacher – how he had told us that a rainbow was the sign of God's promise to man, that as long as the earth endures, seedtime and harvest, cold and heat, summer and winter, day and night, shall not cease. And, as I watched the rainbow, I felt for a moment curiously uplifted and blessed.

That detail in the newspaper today about Dr Morell, Hitler's doctor. Since 1942, it seems, Hitler received an intravenous injection of a stimulant before he got out of bed. Probably his 'pep' injection was cocaine or amphetamines. How easy it would have been for a noble doctor to have bumped Adolf off. So many lives could have been saved. I would call that ethical murder.

There is no question that it would be easy to murder a patient – as Dr Glas did. If I did so, for instance, I'd probably 'get away with it'. The doctor is not obliged to notify the coroner of a sudden or unexplained death. As for getting a second doctor to co-sign a cremation certificate, that would be a formality. No wonder Pliny complained that the physician was the only citizen who could kill another with sovereign impunity, and Hippocrates insisted that, 'Wherever a doctor cannot do good he must be kept from doing harm.'

March 20th

I was moved. I thought Edith had forgotten my birthday but this Monday morning she brought me a most acceptable gift. I didn't spoil her pleasure in giving me the present by telling her that she had mistaken the date.

'My father was alive when I was forty,' Edith related. 'He celebrated by bringing into the house a second-hand Singer sewing machine.'

She had chosen for me, to my astonishment, a print of a Turner water-colour. These days they are becoming increasingly better at producing full colour reproductions. I will frame it and put it on the wall behind my desk.

'I thought with your artistic tastes you would like it,' Edith opined with evident satisfaction.

I continued to thank her warmly. I indicated how touched I was that she had remembered that I had been a March baby. In response, typically, she said critically, 'You need a haircut. You are beginning to resemble one of those shaggy-haired artists yourself. It doesn't do. Not for a doctor, it don't.'

After she had returned to her patch in the kitchen I examined the Turner water-colour closely. It portrayed a lone dog on a deserted beach, facing the immensity of the sea. Turner had painted the sea dark with the suggestions of night and a sky streaked with the blood colour of dawn. The dog's jaw was conspicuously open, its head raised so that the creature appeared to be howling at the new day arriving. It seemed to me to be a lament that nothing could arrest the progress of time, how we must all grow older, become 40, then 50, then 60, then 70, and afterwards, wither and die. The dog was hurling its cosmic protest at the tyrant Time. How apt that Edith had given me this painted metaphor for my time-conscious birthday. But then I spotted the very small lettered title below the scene: *Dawn after the Shipwreck*. I had misinterpreted the picture. The dog was howling (and waiting) for its lost master. Turner's title had transformed this great water-colour into a sentimental story.

This afternoon I visited the Cypriot hairdresser 'Pappy'. He is an excellent barber but a bit too garrulous. He knows I am a doctor so each time I submit to his flying scissors Pappy ventilates at length his hypochondriacal fears and seeks medical advice to allay them.

Rhys once told me that, during his brief time in the RAF, he had learnt how a Service Medical Officer deflected those who inappropriately posed their health problems to him outside the parameters of Sick Quarters. If the RAF doctor happened to be accosted by a symptom-loaded fellow officer, in the Mess say, he would, as instructed, simply say, 'Strip.' This blunt imperative would cause the doctor's interlocutor to become strangely mute.

I could not brusquely command Pappy to strip should he plague me with medical questions but, this afternoon, as he decorated my shoulders with the usual flowing white gown, I attempted to choreograph masterfully our forthcoming conversation.

'What do you think, Pappy,' I asked, 'about the McCarthy anti-red crusade that's in full swing in the USA?'

'I've read about it in the papers,' Pappy answered.

My pre-emptive ploy seemed to work. 'We're a bit paranoiac here in Britain too,' Pappy continued. 'In the very chair you're occupying only yesterday I had a nutter who told me he had dreamt the Russians sent planes over London and dropped sweets not bombs.'

'That's not too bad,' I suggested.

'Only when the kids ran to pick the sweets up and unwrap them they exploded in their faces.'

Unfortunately, the facial wounds suffered by the dreamt-up children reminded Pappy of his brother's medical condition. 'He eats too many sweets, you know, doctor. Could that be the cause of his terrible diarrhoea? Or is it due to stress?'

I thought of the ancient Egyptian sculpture that portrayed a bull defaecating under the stress of being attacked by a lion. Before I could comment, Pappy, wielding his scissors with increasing speed, snip snip snip, turned his monologue to its natural destination, its self's centre.

'I tend to suffer from wind myself,' he confided. 'Could that be nerves, doctor? Could it run in the family? My brother suffers reverse waves in his stomach and bowels.'

Perceptible greyness in my hair now settled upon the barber's white gown. I can't countenance the fact that I am forty, middle-aged. The young fear life; the old fear death. At this transitional juncture, do I fear both? So many things I need to learn before the veteran years arrive. So many things held to be valuable during the discarded years now seem meaningless. That old Zen saying, for instance, that I once thought so wise: 'To a man who knows nothing, mountains are mountains, waters are waters and trees are trees. But when he has studied and knows a little, mountains are no longer mountains, waters no longer waters, trees no longer trees. But when he has thoroughly understood, mountains are once again mountains, waters are waters and trees are trees.'

It was during my convalescence from my breakdown that the psychiatrist at Westminster Hospital introduced me to that Zen homily. Whatever he was trying to say to me escapes me now. I'm baffled, unless he was trying to comfort me, a vexed student, by indicating that fruit becomes sweeter as it ripens. During that time of personal turbulence I had wondered whether I should venture away from the path of medicine towards God knows where. (There was no destination.) Mother had just died and I was not well. I had the continual sense of falling, of clutching at some hand to restrain me.

'Anything else, sir?' asked Pappy, referring to Durex, as he helped me out of the white gown.

All the way home I kept thinking that at forty a man should renew himself, take a new direction. Should I attempt to take the infinite risk of getting married and subsequently suffer the encroachment on my solitude and liberty – not to mention having to endure the regular sweat and musk of sex?

I am reconciled to the fact that I shall never get married. At one time, I thought about my cousin, Marjorie, as a possible loving partner when her husband got killed during the Arnhem parachute jump. I thought of waiting a year or so before travelling to Liverpool to make true contact again. I didn't want to arrive in the middle of her grief. I wrote, to her, of course, letters of regret, and with the passing of the months letters of fond ambiguity. I was surprised how soon she became engaged again. Wartime, wartime. Too late, I learnt that patience can be a vice.

I cannot change the direction of my life. I must go straight on. My medical practice is rewarding enough. Medicines and drugs may be the same but patients are different from each other. True, most of them present with functional ailments and it is not easy to convince a hypochondriac that his or her symptoms are a manifestation of self-distrust. As we grow older how many of us trust our own bodies? One thing I miss since the NHS came into being is that I no longer have the opportunity to feel that rare, satisfactory glow of charity when I've not charged a poor patient.

'No, it's OK, Mr Smith. Don't worry about it. No problem.' No charity, no halo. But from that point of view the NHS offers more gains than losses. I'm glad I'm not like Charlie F. though I know a greater freedom is given to a man without convictions. I'm not one who, to find himself, has to lose himself first.

March 23rd
There is something old-fashioned about the old Cosmo restaurant. It is as if the clock had stopped, not in 1950 but in pre-First World War Vienna. On the wall are prints of one of our local refugee artists, Topolski, and one has the feeling of not being in England. This is partly due to the foreignness of the waiters and waitresses. Before they left their country they probably had been violin or cello players in some great Austrian orchestra or professors of Ichthyology. The menu, too, suggests Vienna: Rheinische Sauerbraten with dumplings and red cabbage; or Wiener Schnitzel; or Zwiebel Hockbraten; or Zwiebel Rosbraten Viennoise; or Karlsbraten Veal Goulash. And those who eat at the restaurant are frequently not British.

Last night, for example, the man at the next table, who could not pronounce his 'r's was surely a successful refugee. The waiter stood, pad and biro in hand, waiting for the customer to order from the menu.

'Uh-huh,' he finally asked, 'is it weal goulash?'
'Of course it's veal,' the waiter said, baffled.
'I said weal not veal,' the customer pronounced. 'If it's not weal I don't want it.'
'It is veal.'
'But weal goulash?'
'Yes, sir, it's real.'
'The goulash is weal. And it's veal?'
'What?'
'It's not pork?'
'No.'

'I don't want pork.'

'It's not pork.'

'Pork I don't want. Not if it's a weal goulash.'

'If it's written on the menu veal, sir, it's veal. And if it's written goulash it's real goulash.'

The customer once more read through the menu and the waiter waited.

'I'll have veal goulash,' he eventually commanded.

I paid my bill and decided to complete my meal in the annexe where I discovered one small table unoccupied. The ambience was quite different. It was only a few steps from the main restaurant to its adjacent annexe but, in taking them, one moved from the Past to the Present.

I was enjoying an apple strudel with a cup of coffee and trying to make sense of an article I was reading in *The Lancet*, when a polite young man asked if he might join me – most of the chairs at other tables had been taken. I put *The Lancet* to one side. So many articles in the medical journals I can't understand these days; specialisation has brought with it a jargon language of its own. It will surely get worse in future. It is no longer a question of artist and scientist belonging to different cultures: doctors can't fully understand doctors, scientist cannot speak to scientist. It has been said that when Freud and Einstein met they got on famously with each other. Freud asserted that this was so because he didn't talk about psychoanalysis and Einstein refrained from discussing physics. 'He is cheerful, sure of himself and agreeable,' Freud said of Einstein. 'He understands as much about psychology as I do about physics so we had a very pleasant talk.'

The recent case history of a man found sprawled semi-conscious on the pavement outside the Heart Hospital in Queens Square, serves as a parable about over-specialisation in medicine. The man was carried into the Heart Hospital where the medical attendants felt helpless to deal with him and suggested he be taken across the Square to the nearby general hospital.

There, in the Casualty Department, the registrar was soon on the phone to the registrar of the Heart Hospital to ask, 'What do you want us to do with the patient who fell out of one of your windows?'

'You're a doctor,' the young man who had joined me at the table suddenly said, pointing at *The Lancet*.

He introduced himself to me as Peter Dawson and told me almost at once that he had recently begun his first junior job in a literary agency.

'That must be interesting,' I said vaguely.

'Friends of our authors are forever writing children's stories illustrated by friends of their friends,' he sighed.

'You could represent some of the people here,' I said, trying to make polite conversation. 'Quite a few who frequent this place have something to do with books.'

'Ah yes,' agreed Peter Dawson. 'That fellow over there, whom everybody calls Gerald the Hat, he steals them. He's the authors' friend. Foyle's may lose out but the authors still get their ten per cent.'

Our thin conversation halted momentarily when the waitress came over to take his order. 'Same as usual, Peter?' she asked familiarly. 'A coffee and a spam sandwich?'

The waitress departed and Peter Dawson told me that one of his clients was a doctor. 'They're going to produce a play of his on the Home Service but he's resisting being edited.'

'Edited?'

'Yes, they've told him they can only allow him one 'bloody' per half hour on Saturday Night Theatre.'

'You're joking.'

'No.'

Our conversation was dramatically interrupted, this time by the stagey entrance into the annexe of a tall, red-haired fellow who shouted, in a sergeant-major's voice, 'Come outside,' and added several excremental expletives certainly disallowed by the Drama Department of the BBC. He was addressing Gerald the

Hat who simply objected quietly, 'It's raining, Ginger.'

'Come outside, you pisser,' screamed Ginger.

'Calm down, Ginger.'

The hefty, red-haired fellow – evidently known as Ginger to his acquaintances – addressed the now attentive clientele of the Cosmo annexe.

'I put this thieving bastard up last night because he had nowhere to sleep and this morning the shit buzzed off with my shirts. In fact, he's got one of mine on now.'

'I haven't.'

'Take it off.'

'It's not your shirt.'

'That's my shirt, take it off. TAKE IT OFF.'

In a somewhat tremulous voice Gerald appealed to the curious spectators. 'This is my old blue shirt. I've had it for years.'

'Smells as if he's had it on for years,' someone interjected.

'You better come outside. I'm goin' to break your bloody neck.'

Ginger then slapped Gerald the Hat's face resoundingly and once more invited his sitting victim to settle matters in the street. Gerald merely laughed, though without merriment. When Ginger threw his hat over the coffee counter, he laughed even louder. It was as if he could not stop laughing. He was incontinent with laughter.

One of the waiters interposed himself between the two men. Ginger managed to spit on Gerald's convulsing face.

'Out,' said the waiter to Ginger. 'Out. Beat it or I'll call the police.'

Gerald the Hat ceased laughing. 'S'alright,' he muttered. 'No need.'

Evidently he wanted no truck with the police. The red-haired man turned on his heel and rushed out into the street. The hum of conversation started up again. Some kind person retrieved the thrown hat and gave it to its owner who, white-faced, stood up and said to us, the jury, 'I didn't nick any shirts. I don't nick shirts.' He sat down and lit a cigarette.

More and more people crowded into the annexe, which began to smell of wet mackintoshes. I was about to leave when Rhys came in. At first, I thought he would ignore me. Instead he drew up a chair and I introduced him to the young literary agent. He more or less ignored Peter Dawson and said to me urgently, 'I'm worried, really worried, Robbie. I've just come from Richmond. She's near the edge.'

I do not recall ever having seen Rhys so agitated. Peter Dawson, from time to time, searched my face as Rhys obsessively continued to speak of Amy Middleton's desperation, her suicidal intent. Impulsively, I pulled out of my pocket the card Charlie Forster had given me. I hesitated. Freddie Hill had plenty of gynaecological experience.

'What have you got there?' queried Rhys.

Was it folly on my part? I passed the card to Rhys wordlessly. Peter Dawson, perhaps troubled, hailed the waiter. My friend scrutinised the card, then said, 'Thank you, Robbie.'

March 25th

Freebooter won the Grand National. Why didn't I put a fiver on the horse? I heard someone say that on the way coming home from Trafalgar Square, upstairs on a number 13 bus. I had been to the National Gallery. I stood before the self-portrait of Elizabeth Vigée-Lebrun for a long time. I don't know how I ever imagined she resembled Yvonne. Yvonne's face has much more mystery and melancholy in it. Simply, Yvonne is incomparably more beautiful.

March 26th

I had so much pleasure from my visit to the National Gallery yesterday. I respond more to paintings than I do to music. I am transported, though, by the Schubert record Bloomberg gave me – its duality of feeling, the profound sorrow of the composer, aware of our life cycle's inevitable conclusion and his simultaneous resigned celebration of that fact.

I did not tell the truth when I informed Anton Bloomberg that I admired the music of Wagner. Why did I tell Bloomberg that fib? When I called Wagner, that notorious anti-semite, a great man, did I do it deliberately to provoke Bloomberg, to needle him? No, I don't care too much for bluster and grandeur in music. That accordionist playing 'Barbara Allen' the other night, when I was walking away from the Plurabelle with Charlie, touched deeper fathoms in my mind than the blastings of a Wagner or a Berlioz or a Mahler. I am entranced when I hear a single flute being played in a night train or a mouth organ in a tented field while camping or at picnic-time.

In 1930, I went abroad for the first time with my mother – to Venice. My mother wanted to look at some paintings by Veronese in a certain church. Because a service was going on we moved quietly, trying not to draw attention to ourselves. In any case we were hidden in the shadows behind the great pillars. We did not listen to the priest or to the responses of the small congregation. The church was large and spacious, the people there few and we concentrated on our secular and visual purposes. Then, startled, we heard the violin. The music pure and serious. We sat on the wooden chairs captivated by a Bach partita, played by a solo violin, the music of calm space enclosed by solemn stone. The music seemed to reveal the secrets of the impossible.

Music rarely touches me like that, so intensely. Bloomberg, I gather – I must stop writing now. Rhys is at the front door ready for our Sunday afternoon chess game. We are friends again.

Later

Rhys is too much involved with Amy Middleton. I'm glad, though, that he persuaded her to give him the cyanide phial, which is now safe, locked up with the other dangerous drugs, in my surgery. Rhys persists in speaking of her like one smitten.

'She's a really open person and sweet-natured. Her husband has more or less abandoned her. He's having it off in Germany. She's on her own, Robbie.'

'Not always,' I said.

Anyway, it seems Amy Middleton has made an appointment to see Charlie Forster and Co. at Harley Street. Rhys, persuasive as ever, had made a deal with her. 'She was as emotional as Bette Davis and Barbara Stanwyck combined,' he said. He had given her the Harley Street card I had given him in exchange for the cyanide phial, which he has now given me!

At the front door, as he was leaving, Rhys said, 'You've been very helpful. The sea comes in and the sea goes out but I won't forget it, Robbie. I know your attitude about abortion and legality. I know what you've done goes against the grain. Amy asked me to express her gratitude.'

'I've done nothing,' I said, alarmed.

I had passed a visiting card on to him, that was all. 'I don't want to be implicated,' I insisted.

'Of course not. Don't worry,' Rhys assured me.

I nodded. He smiled.

'How did you get on in the Prompt Corner tournament?' I asked.

'I lost,' he said. 'But I'm winning with Amy.'

After Rhys had gone the house became itself again – an emptiness at the heart of it – like the room upstairs once occupied by my mother. And I felt restless. That was an hour ago and I still feel restless, hungry for some action. I despise myself because, as Charlie reckons, I don't take risks. It's stupid of me to feel anxious just because I handed Rhys Charlie's visiting card.

I don't know. I'm not entirely satisfied with the Sisyphus routine of my life – this routine, day after day, week after week, month after month, of seeing patients, most of them complaining of imaginary ills or with serious diseases that are untreatable; playing chess with Rhys every Sunday; Edith always fussing in the same way: 'your shoes aren't clean, you

should wear a vest in winter, cast not a clout till May is out.'
Christ, the sheer regularity of it all makes my life almost absurd
unless I choose to bring myself more alive by risking paths of
unpredictability.

Yes, I'm hungry for fresh action. I remember how the
Reverend Gregorius took the cyanide. He was accompanied by
Dr Glas who had recommended it. He swallowed it down with a
drink of water, believing it was good for his heart. Then Dr Glas
heard Anton Bloomberg's glass fall and shatter on the floor; he
saw Bloomberg's arm drop limply down and his Jewish face sink
down towards his chest with his fish-eyes widely open.

I must not. I dare not.

March 31st
I recognised the diminutive, backward-sloping writing on the
envelope immediately – the envelope itself was more elegant
than the scrimpy brown ones which my unwelcome anonymous
correspondent has previously sent me. The postmark was too
blurred for me to decipher; the contents of the letter more crazy,
more disturbing than before: 'My dear Dr Robert Simmonds,' it
began, 'I dare you, this coming Saturday morning at 11 a.m. to
meet me near the grave of George Eliot in Highgate Cemetery. I
shall unmask myself to you, you the source of my disgust. I am
friend to the star of the nether world whom I have invoked to
perish your mind and to paralyse your feet.'

I've been thinking of the patients I have had who have been
difficult or odd or whom I've offended in some way. I recalled
my recent altercation with Mrs Townsend. She complained of
migrainous attacks and has not visited my surgery since she
accused me of not listening to her story. 'You're ice-cold,' she
said, accusing me. She was surely not the sort of person, though,
who would send such an unbalanced note. Besides, the earlier
anonymous letters had been coming through the post long before
our trivial quarrel. No, it must be someone nearer the festering

borders of insanity. Who? And should I show this bizarre threat to someone else, to the police?

Then it came to me: tomorrow, Saturday, was April 1st, April Fools' Day. Someone was genuinely trying, perhaps, to urge me to visit George Eliot's grave (why George Eliot?) and to make a fool of me. It was all a practical joke: someone wanted to exert his or her sense of power by disturbing me and causing me to go on a fool's errand to Highgate.

I threw the note into the fire.

April 1st

I wouldn't have thought of walking to George Eliot's grave in Highgate Cemetery if it hadn't been one of those spring mornings the English poets have been lyrical about. Sunlight flooded the rooms of our house and was particularly assertive in the breakfast room while I read the morning newspaper. Afterwards, for a few minutes, I stood at the window thinking of the sorrows of the great world, the Cold War. Our own government, according to the *Manchester Guardian*, is planning a sixth sinister atomic centre at Aldermaston in Berkshire – not a hundred miles away from the Freda Dixon Institute, Nightingale Manor. History is a ghost of the Present.

Outside was birdsong and not one cloud bolted across the blue sky so I decided to go for a walk. April Fool or not, why should I eschew Highgate Cemetery? Some years had passed since I had visited that 'Victorian Valhalla' as it has been called. Would I be able to seek out George Eliot's grave when 170,000 others lay in their ruins there? I recalled it was not far from the conspicuous monument of Karl Marx.

I discovered that there was a West and an East side to the cemetery. Since the West gate was closed I took the available East route and strolled between great, neglected vaults and funeral sculptures half hidden by encroaching foliage, fallen columns and concealed graves. I could not help recalling how the *Hampstead and Highgate Express* had reported that witches practised their strange black magic rituals at midnight in these morbid precincts. Doubtless, necrophilic vandals also loved to run amok here during the darkest hours.

I came to a fork in the pathway and, as I hesitated, wondering whether to go right or left, a group of what I took to be students appeared. Resolutely they pursued the left direction and, instinctively, I followed them. Soon the muscular monument of Karl Marx came into view and those ahead of me stopped to survey his huge, hypertrophied bust. Opposite Marx's monument I discovered the grave of Herbert Spencer. Beautiful serendipity: Marx and Spencer! Marx who called upon the workers of the world to unite and Herbert Spencer who told the world that 'to play billiards well was a sign of an ill-spent youth'!

Seeking George Eliot's grave I clambered up a slope past ivy-covered tombs, leaving the group of students chatting in the shadow of Karl Marx. At last I stumbled on what I was searching for. I looked at my wrist-watch. I had timed it pretty well: four minutes to eleven o'clock. Nobody was about. I glanced quickly at the inscription on the resting place of Mary Ann Evans, better known as George Eliot, before walking a cricket pitch away where I loitered and lit up a cigarette. After all, there was just an outside chance that my crazy correspondent would turn up to see me being hoaxed. I resolved to hang on for a few minutes or so.

Nothing happened. I watched a lone butterfly stagger across this quiet stadium of souls and having finished my cigarette I was about to leave this sunlit, bushy spot when a youngish woman in a long coat appeared. Alert now, I felt a lump in my oesophagus. She looked familiar. She glanced at me with transparent hostility before stopping and staring at the green shallows about George Eliot's grave.

Definitely. I had seen her before. Though twenty yards away, I could see that this rather tubby woman wore no make-up, was spectacled, rosy-cheeked and had brown hair tied back in a bun. Surely a patient of mine? Then I remembered how a young woman, very much like her, had visited my consulting room just before Christmas and asked me to sign the back of a couple of passport photos saying that this was a true image of etc. etc. I peered at her again. It was her. I was almost certain it was her. But why should this person send me psychotic, threatening, anonymous notes?

She gazed towards me, unsmiling. I would let her speak first. I could see she was uneasy because of my motionless, statuesque presence. Sure enough, she turned and walked away, aiming for the main pathway that allowed visitors legitimate passage between the muddled shambles of the cemetery.

I was not going to let her get away before I challenged her. If I was mistaken, so be it. I rehearsed in my mind what I would say to her. 'Aren't you a patient of mine?' I'd say. And if she acknowledged that this was so, I would directly ask her why she sent me anonymous, wanton threats. She was glancing back every now and then and quickened her pace. But with inquisitorial determination I walked faster too. She increased her speed again though she was hampered by her long coat. I would have to run to catch up with her but when she reached the fork in the pathway where a knot of several people had gathered, she stopped and allowed me to approach.

'If you don't stop following me, I'll scream,' she almost shouted. 'Go away.'

I was close to her now, very close, and suddenly I realised where I had previously seen her. At the Cosmo. She was one of the Cosmo crowd. She was staring, as if in horror, at my face, my scarred face.

'I'm sorry,' I said.

'Bugger off,' she said.

I felt such a silly ass. Other people were looking our way. What a faux-pas!

'I've made a mistake,' I said.

'You sure have, mister.'

I noticed one of my shoelaces was undone and I bent down

while she walked away athletically. When she was out of sight I, too, ambled out of Highgate Cemetery, away from Death's mouldering holograph.

April 4th

Mrs Levy attended my morning surgery. She had heard from a relative in New York about a new wonder drug, cortisone, that could cure arthritis. Her relative had enclosed a newspaper cutting with her letter.

'Let me read you,' Mrs Levy said. 'It says that on the 21st September, 1948, Dr Philip S. Hench of the Mayo Clinic in Rochester, gave cortisone to a bedridden woman, crippled by rheumatoid arthritis, and within a week his patient was happily walking down the main street of Rochester on a shopping expedition.' Mrs Levy put down the cutting on my desk. 'What do you think of that, doctor?'

'I know about cortisone, Mrs Levy. I intend to refer to it in the talk I'm to give at the Broadhurst Gardens meeting later this month. I hope you'll come and ... '

'Listen,' Mrs Levy interrupted me, 'if it worked for a bedridden woman what would it do for my back? I could become a trapeze artist.'

'The situation is ... '

'You know that newspaper report goes on to say how this Hench doctor tried out this cortisone only six months ago on fourteen more rheumatic arthritis cripples. Afterwards, wheelchairs were discarded, crutches thrown away. I think this great American doctor should get a page in the Old Testament.'

'Cortisone is not generally available this side of the Atlantic,' I told Mrs Levy.

'Not available?'

'No. Besides, Mrs Levy, you have osteo-arthritis, not rheumatoid arthritis.'

'My luck,' she said. 'If I sold lamps the sun would shine at night.'

It will be wonderful if cortisone does prove to be an effective remedy for severe rheumatoid arthritis. At present, the tapping noise of sticks on the road to Lourdes is too loud.

*

After this morning's surgery I went into the empty waiting room. Someone had left behind last week's *Hampstead and Highgate Express*. On its Arts page a photograph of the Israeli pianist Shoshana Shamir caught my attention. I recognised her. This was the companion of Anton Bloomberg whom I had seen in the foyer of the Embassy Theatre. She was to give, I noted, a recital of Beethoven sonatas at Hampstead's Burgh House. Well, Bloomberg not only liked music but also musicians!

She did not resemble an Israeli with her long coal-coloured falling tresses that extended below her shoulders. A number of Palestine-born Israelis – Sabras I think they call them – have frequented the Cosmo recently and their bearing and appearance is pleasanter than most of the refugees who look pale, darker and less athletic.

Still, it's not the Israeli pianist nor even Anton Bloomberg himself who, more than fitfully, occupy my thoughts. It is Yvonne. Day in, day out, she comes to mind, lovely conjuration, during these regular moments of reverie – especially when I lie in bed at night before I go to sleep and in the morning when I awake. No one knows this, no one at all – unless it be my doppel-ganger, Dr Glas!

The other night – yes I shall confess here – the other night I woke up pleasured, my pyjama trousers sticky and wet. I also felt disgraced. I smelt of the swimming baths, of chlorine. I had to get up and change.

The peculiar thing was that in my illicit joyful dream I had lain not with Yvonne but with Amy Middleton! I had been embracing and fucking one whom I find worthless.

I sensed that I had somehow contaminated Yvonne, my pure one.

April 5th

When I returned from my afternoon round Edith met me in the hall.

'Mr Hugh Fisher is here to see you,' she said. 'I've put him in the waiting room though he says it's not a medical matter. He's been here nearly an hour.'

'Hugh Fisher?'

I ushered the effete, gangling Hugh Fisher into my surgery. 'I should have phoned you,' he said, even before taking a seat, 'but I wanted to talk to you face to face about postponing your lecture to our Broadhurst Gardens group.'

I'd opened the door for Hugh Fisher so that he had gone ahead of me. I was somewhat taken aback when he proceeded to walk to the other side of my desk, selecting my usual seat. I took the patient's chair.

'You see,' Fisher said apologetically, 'Frank Middleton is over here from Germany because his wife is in hospital. He says it'll be difficult for him to return in May. He'd like to deliver his prepared lecture while he's here, if that's possible.'

'His wife is in hospital?'

'In the St Lucy clinic, I understand. Had a miscarriage. They're both very upset, I gather.'

Hugh Fisher related with prosaic exactitude how the committee had been called for an emergency meeting to discuss whether they should postpone my talk; the time of the meeting; who was at the meeting; how X said this and Y said that; and how Yvonne Bloomberg had voted not to delay my talk until May.

'The others on the committee, including our treasurer, Clive Silver,' Hugh Fisher said earnestly, 'felt that to hear Mr Middleton talk about the Nazi war criminals, of whom he has intimate knowledge – *intimate* knowledge – would be of great interest to our membership.'

'Yes, of course,' I said.

'We're all set to roneo a notice announcing the change in our lecture schedule and to send it out, if you agree.'

'Sure. It's OK.'

'As a matter of fact the May lecture always follows our AGM so you'll have a bumper audience then.'

'No problem,' I repeated.

'Thank you. Thank you.'

I accompanied him to the front door. In the hall, I asked, 'How's Yvonne?'

He turned towards me and a smile lit his face, changing it remarkably. 'I didn't have much time to talk to her after the Emergency Committee meeting. She shot off. But I saw her last Sunday,' he said cheerfully. 'Anton was busy. So Yvonne and I took the dog for a walk.'

I closed the front door. Edith, curious, was at the entrance to the kitchen. 'Tea's ready,' she said.

'Edith,' I replied. 'We must change the patient's chair in my surgery. It's too low. It's not comfortable.'

April 6th

This morning, entering my surgery, I encountered Edith carrying withered flowers as she came out. Flustered, as if caught in some rare profane act, she exclaimed, 'Oh, oh. You need fresh flowers. I'll pick some from the garden.' And she hurried away as if on a vital mission. What was wrong? Why such haste?

I discovered my journals on my desk. Usually I'm meticulous about locking them up after I have completed an entry. I must have forgotten to do so last night. I wonder if Edith has been glancing at these pages.

I am not anxious for anybody to read my journals other than my older self. If I'm not around in fifty years time I wouldn't care a fig then. Mind you, the way the USSR and the USA seem intent on colliding with each other, nobody may be around long decades before the year 2000. We could all be radioactive carrion for the surviving flies.

*

I can't help wondering what sort of person I might have become had I not chosen to be a doctor. At school I was always told that I had a considerable literary talent. Could I have become a professional writer? I don't envy those lay-about artist types who frequent the Cosmo. They waste so much time – long evenings in, long evenings out. And probably most of them are deluded about the worth of their talent. They occupy so little of the world's space and are so self-directed.

Probably all caged birds sing as an alternative to dreaming.

I've just finished writing up my clinical notes. So many patients this morning. The priests are fools who contend that suffering has a purpose. I remember Darwin's dry answer when one of that breed pronounced that God created this multitudinous world with a purpose in mind. He said, 'I cannot persuade myself to believe in a beneficent God who caused Ichneumonidae to exist with the express intention of their feeding within the living body of caterpillars.'

When I was an adolescent I happened on Llewelyn Powys's *The Pathetic Fallacy* at the public library. I took it home and wrote out some lines from that book which meant a great deal to me. At that time I was looking forward to beginning my medical studies. Powys magisterially argued, 'Not even a Pharaoh, a Caesar or a Tamburlaine can reconcile himself to an existence inconsequent and empty of meaning. The egoism of the species is involved. Let the lives of pismires, of pygargs, be without significance but not those of cardinal man.' When I became a medical student I inscribed those lines in one of my medical textbooks. (I have the book still and I've just copied it out.)

I was confident then that medicine was an altruistic pursuit – 'my purpose in life'. It was a way, too, to confront the mystery of the Enigma. Now? I don't know. Perhaps if I addressed the stone Sphinx and ordered it to speak, it would simply say, 'Mama.'

*

April 9th

When Rhys crashed in for our usual sabbath afternoon chess game, I suggested that we give chess a miss and sample instead Frank Middleton's lecture at Broadhurst Gardens.

'Frank Middleton's giving a lecture?'

I showed him the crude, roneoed leaflet: STOP PRESS. THE NAZI HUMAN GUINEA PIGS, *a lecture by the celebrated Nazi inquisitor, Frank Middleton, at the Broadhurst Gardens Centre, April 9th, 3pm.*

'Nazi human guinea pigs? The guinea pigs are Nazis?' Rhys wise-cracked.

I wanted to go because I knew Yvonne would be present. She would already be in the hall.

'I wouldn't mind hearing Frank Middleton in action,' I said.

'F. Middleton thinks himself one helluva panjandrum,' said Rhys. 'He thinks he can defy gravity. He deigned to pop in to see Amy when she was in the St Lucy Clinic and stayed, like Royalty, for two and a half minutes. Didn't even bring a bunch of urine-provoking dandelions. I believe he imagines I'm Amy's White Knight.'

'Well you are, aren't you?'

'Anyway Amy's home and dry now – well wet, but OK.'

I was thankful that there had been no complications. Whatever else, Freddie Hill had been a competent junior gynaecologist before he gave it up for General Practice. I was relieved that it was all over. And I could claim credit for giving Rhys Charlie Forster's card.

'The Nazis' human guinea pigs should be interesting,' I persuaded Rhys.

'Yeh, should be a romp and a hoot,' Rhys hesitated. 'OK. Let's go and hear the bucolic alcoholic. Bet you he'll read a prepared paper with careful, spontaneous asides which he has typed in – bet you. How long do you think it'll last? We could play chess after we come out of that Broadhurst Gardens torture-chamber.'

'We'd better leave now, right away,' I said. 'It's ten to three.'

'With any luck we'll miss half of it,' Rhys said.

As it happened the car wouldn't start. I pulled out the choke, tried again and again. My Morris Minor sounded as if it had croup.

'You've flooded the engine, you genius, you Malcolm Campbell.'

We had to wait patiently before I dared try the ignition again. Rhys chatted about Amy. 'Did you know she's a keen ornithologist?'

'What?'

'Ornithologist. Bird-watcher. Expert. Christ, Robbie, what are you grinning for? You can't tell a kestrel from a skylark.'

The engine at last consented to come to life as I frenetically pressed the accelerator up and down.

'Terrific,' commented Rhys.

We arrived at Broadhurst Gardens at half past three. We missed, of course, Hugh Fisher's introductory remarks and, at a guess, probably nearly half of Frank Middleton's lecture. Rhys and I managed to find two seats at the rear of the small, crowded hall. On the raised platform, on either side of the gesticulating Frank Middleton, sat Hugh Fisher and Clive Silver. It took me some time to spot Yvonne. She occupied a gangway chair next to Anton Bloomberg. Husband and wife together. Had their far from customary togetherness any significance?

Peering over his spectacles, Frank Middleton said, 'When the State cultivates the paranoid notion that certain members of the community are dangerous, degraded, and sub-human – be they Jews, be they the insane or criminals – then the likelihood that doctors will be pressed into the service of demoniacal agents becomes a real possibility...'

That the Bloombergs were together did not mean they were in harmonious accord. Didn't Hugh Fisher inform me that a week ago he, along with Yvonne, had taken the dog for a walk because 'Anton was busy'? Yes, busy as likely as not, with that Israeli woman, deceiving his unsuspecting, magnanimous wife. I glanced at Rhys; a mirthless pensive expression had usurped his customary impish features. I tried to concentrate on what Frank Middleton was saying. He seemed to be directing his gaze at me.

'Conform or die was the dictate of the Nazi regime,' Frank Middleton asserted. 'An attitude that obtained for them, doctors eminent or otherwise, and that can become operative in any totalitarian country. The majority of doctors in Nazi Germany, in fact, could adapt themselves to the regime without contravening the Hippocratic oath. Most of the 90,000 doctors in Hitler's Germany felt that to protest was useless, and closed their eyes to flagrant medico-ethical abuses. Only some 350 committed crimes... '

As Middleton outlined the chilling nature of these criminal misdemeanours, I imagined myself as a German doctor. Would I have conformed? I looked again at the figure of Anton Bloomberg. There were other Jews in the audience, quite a number I guessed, and a couple of them wore little black caps on their heads. Then, suddenly, I felt a little giddy – though only for a moment.

'...the amount of suffering they caused was fantastic and horrifying. They engaged in experimental work with drugs and in surgery. They did low-pressure and cooling experiments, frequently killing their human guinea pigs without a qualm. They carried out fearful tests on the possibility of drinking sea water. They experimented with viruses such as those that cause hepatitis. And also with typhus vaccines. They perpetrated unspeakable experiments on Jewish twins, they... '

'I must get out of here,' I whispered to Rhys for, ridiculously, I felt giddy again.

'They worked as death doctors with mustard gas. They tried out methods of sterilising human beings. Their blood lust... '

I rose and the floor tilted. I had to get out. I was going to be sick. I was aware that the people occupying the wooden chairs in rows anterior to us had twisted their heads – their wrath-kindled heads back to front. I managed to blurt a quiet 'excuse me', as I

136

passed bony knees. Rhys followed. Outside, across the road from John Barnes' store, Rhys asked, 'You OK? You went so white.'

'Something I ate,' I said. 'I felt nauseous.'

'Gawd,' pronounced Rhys. 'What a sensitive doctor. Couldn't stomach what Middleton was describing.'

'Course not,' I insisted. 'It wasn't that.'

'Anybody would think you were a Jew,' said Rhys.

'Let's get to the car,' I said.

I hope Yvonne didn't notice me leave. She probably did not know that I had even bothered to come this Sunday afternoon to the Broadhurst Gardens Centre.

I drove Rhys home. I did not feel like playing chess. Instead I've added this entry to my journal.

Five minutes ago the telephone called me away from my dinner. It was Yvonne. Hugh Fisher, from the platform, had seen me leave. He thought that I had staggered out and wondered whether I was ill. 'I'm fine,' I said. 'I felt a little nauseous for a while but I'm OK now.'

'I was worried,' she said.

'Worried?'

'Well, I know how doctors sometimes neglect themselves.'

'No, no,' I said. 'Doctors live a very long time because they avoid taking any of their medicines.'

Yvonne laughed. 'Well, I hope you'll come to a party at our place that we're giving for Hugh Fisher. It'll be for his thirtieth birthday.'

'Hugh Fisher?'

'Yes, on April 29th. I'll send you a card, Robbie. Do come. We never have a chance to talk.'

'Yes, I'll come,' I said. 'Thanks for thinking of me.'

Hugh Fisher? Giving a party for him? Yvonne and he seem to be connected these days. Taking a walk together. Conferring at committee meetings. Surely she does not relish his company? He has a job in the Accounts department of the BBC and his dolorous conversation is that of a second division accountant. He might be good-natured but I have the sense that he is one well-versed in expediency. His very facial expression with his high, arching eyebrows seems to belong to one perpetually perplexed through being consistently purged. And he is tactless. He had the impudence, now I come to think of it, to march into my surgery, to circumvent the barrier of my desk and to seat himself in my chair, leaving me to flounder in the seat opposite him like a miscreant. That was an insensitive act. A small indication of someone too self-directed.

Am I being too censorious? Probably. My judgement awry because I still don't feel well. Irritable? The Bloombergs must be on close terms with him for them to host his thirtieth birthday party.

April 13th
All this week I've not been myself. I've woken up much too early and have had to forego too many healing hours of necessary sleep. Each morning I have come down the stairs without my usual legerity. I have experienced brief giddy spells and twice in the last four days I've cut myself shaving. I've had to use up wads of cotton wool to stem the blood flow.

I am aware that cutting oneself while shaving can have a symbolic significance. Last November at a BMA meeting, a prison doctor related how frequently convicts masochistically cut themselves. My cuts, to be sure, were accidents and I'm not a penitent, feeling guilty and trying to punish himself.

April 14th
When I learnt that Michael Butler had died the day before yesterday at Nightingale Manor – Rachel Butler had left a phone message with Edith – I decided to delay visiting the house at Buckland Crescent until after the funeral which, I presume, will take place at Nightingale Manor, at that ornate chapel with its

windows stained with deep rich colour and its blue decorations – not only ceiling and carpet but blue everywhere, suggesting the fake heaven of infinity. Patients, alas, die but doctors should not attend their funerals. Why should we witness and luxuriate in our defeat, celebrate Thanatos's victory? I shall simply send flowers as I always have done when I've lost a patient.

I liked Michael. I admired him – his courage, his curiosity about everything, his breadth of knowledge, his enjoyment in relating compelling stories that he had picked up from arcane sources. Each occasion I visited to give him a morphine injection, his façade of cheerfulness made it easier for me. He was considerate in that way.

Rachel had, has, more ambivalent feelings towards me ever since she realised that one day I was likely to be Michael's executioner. I was the Devil with the hypodermic syringe whom she loathed and yet welcomed. She extended, as it were, an invisible right hand to ward me off, but with her left hand she beckoned me to come nearer. In the event, the morphine I would have finally injected into Michael remains unused, locked up next to that cyanide phial in my surgery. When I visit Rachel, as I shall soon, may I find the right words to console her.

Thanatos. Do we have to begin to say yes to our ultimate destiny of returning to inanimate matter as soon as we reach middle-age? Did Michael, older at 61, by contracting cancer, renounce life too soon? I once heard someone in the Cosmo say, 'Suicide was a way of life in Vienna.' Did Freud, who lived there, soon after the butchery of the First World War, correctly postulate a death instinct? I can't deny our own destructiveness, outward and inward, even if it is expressed minimally, in trivial ways, such as my shaving cuts! I recognise in my patients the ineluctable bipolarity of human nature. Some pugnaciously combat their ailments; others seem resigned, yet unaware of their suicidal tendencies, would vehemently deny that they would really like to wake up dead.

*

Because I continued to feel listless, 'under the weather', and the real weather happened to be pleasantly benign with fleeting April sunlight, I prescribed fresh air for myself. By the time I had climbed to the Whitestone Pond, one of the highest points in London, my head had cleared. I could see across the miles of Heath and further still, beyond the rooftops of the far suburbs, the faint, smudged sky-line of the City's high buildings, including the dome of St Paul's Cathedral. I turned to watch some kids, supervised by absent-minded mothers, sail their toy boats to America or around the Cape of Good Hope. Then, as if some orchestral conductor had raised his arms, the mothers all became alert for a white dog had invaded the pond, bounced and frolicked, almost sinking one of the boats, causing one of the children to howl as if he had been tortured.

I walked away from the fuss, taking the West direction down North End Road, passing the box-like Jack Straw's Castle. When I came to The Old Bull and Bush pub I was transported back through the years. My mother sat in the kitchen shelling peas that 'tinked' as they dropped into a zinc bowl. As she did so she sang the old Victorian music-hall song:

> Come, come,
> Come and make eyes at me
> Down at the Old Bull and Bush...

Near the large, imposing house where a plaque boasted that the dancer Anna Pavlova had once lived there, I passed through the open iron gates into Golders Hill Park. I read somewhere that earlier this century, W.H. Hudson used to stroll regularly here with his literary Hampstead friend, Ernest Rhys, the editor of the Everyman Library. I can understand why these two chums chose this intimate park to walk through. Its green slopes, trees, bushes, ponds, walled flower garden, bandstand and small zoo combine to make it one of the most attractive lesser parks of London. Little did I know that within the next half hour I would experience two unexpected encounters.

First, I observed ahead of me a figure in rags, sprawled full-length on a wooden bench. A greasy, ex-army, khaki balaclava was pulled down on his forehead over his eyebrows and a shabby grey scarf reached above his nostrils. Only the bridge of his nose and a suggestion of an eyelid were visible. As I drew closer I had the impression that this man was not breathing, that this was a constructed Guy Fawkes dummy – not a real human being. If I had been one of those children sailing their boats in the Whitestone Pond, I would have known, indisputably, that here, now, this April afternoon, I had encountered the frightening, primal Bogeyman.

Even as an adult I felt uneasy! I looked around and about for the solace of other reassuring human beings. A few people were walking the other side of the bandstand and, far down the slope, opposite the flower garden, on the expanse of grass, a fellow was trying to raise a kite and another man was watching him. I was now standing directly opposite the figure on the bench. A tramp? He was so motionless. Then it struck me: he was dead. A child's voice cried, 'The bogeyman is dead.' What should I do? Far away the man was still struggling with his kite.

Should I take the tramp's pulse? Alert a park-keeper? Where was the park-keeper? Phone for an ambulance? I began to bend down but drew back quickly when this man in rags with no discernible face perceptibly stirred. One eyelid had opened. One very blue eye stared at me staring at him. He sat up alarmed. 'I'm sorry,' I said and relieved, I walked on. The irony was that I had frightened him. He had seen my scarred face bending towards his and I had become his bogeyman. Just as I had frightened the girl in Highgate Cemetery.

I made my way down the gravel pathway and I noted how the man who had been watching the fellow trying to raise the kite, was now helping him. I crossed the wooden bridge that skirted the duck pond and entered the walled rose garden. And then, there he was – Anton Bloomberg!

They sat close together on a wooden bench beneath the magnolia tree, its new pink and white blossom richly beautiful above their heads. Anton Bloomberg had taken both the pianist's hands in his and was examining them. Quickly I moved to the side, behind the greenery on a high trellis, so that I should not be observed. Bloomberg brought both the hands of Shoshana Shamir to his lips. A gesture of love, or was he more impersonally paying homage to music? I did not wish to be a pathological voyeur. This was a chocolate-box scene. I turned and left the walled garden as swiftly and as quietly as I could.

It seemed to me that I had accidentally stumbled on Anton Bloomberg's and Shoshana Shamir's secret meeting place. Where should lovers not meet but in a rose-garden? Bloomberg was having an affair with the pianist and so betraying his gentle, Gentile wife. It made me angry just to think about it – though, sexually, for the present, it was a solution for Yvonne. But how long would that Israeli stay entangled with him? She would discover his crudity, his simmering violence and then Yvonne would be at his mercy again. From afar, from the little zoo, I heard a peacock screech.

I sat down on a bench not too far away from the empty tennis courts. The daffodils had withered away. They no longer swayed in the small wind, back and fore like praying orthodox Jews. But under the blossoming orchard trees behind me it was bluebells, bluebells, bluebells, my mother's favourite flower. Every spring, she would sooner or later quote that poet-priest, Gerard Manley Hopkins: 'I do not think I have ever seen anything more beautiful than the bluebell...I know the beauty of our Lord by it.'

April 17th

I could put it off no longer. What a grey word 'duty' is. I drove over to the peeling, stucco-clad houses of Buckland Crescent. The Life v Death game for Michael Butler was irrevocably over. There would be no return match. What should I say to his widow? *Navigare necesse est, vivere non necesse.* Would she, like any number of widows in their blacks, whisper, 'My happiness lies in the grave with him'? I didn't think Rachel Butler was that kind of person and would prove to be more buttoned-up, less willing to expose her wound – but one could never tell. My guess was that when I spoke to her, her stiff English upper lip would tremble only for a moment.

I believe they had had a good marriage. Rachel was not a wife who, years back when both were reasonably fit, would have mused, 'If one of us should die, I shall go to Paris.' I fully expected that she would utter the usual widow's litany of self-reproach, 'Doctor, I did not do enough.' How many times have I heard one in mourning, cry out in self-revilement? I suppose new widow or widowerhood is a time for self-examination as well as tearful remembrance.

The house in Buckland Crescent did not resemble one of mourning. Two of the Butler daughters had rallied to their mother and had brought with them their young children who did not walk on tiptoe. I could hear their piping cries even after they were banished to the kitchen.

In the days before the war, the widow would have pulled down the blinds in the front room – where we sat now – shutting out the sun and the noise of the world outside. The neighbours, too, out of respect, would have blinded their windows. And last year I had to visit a Jewish family in mourning. Primitively, they had rent their clothes, and covered all the mirrors in the house – not just the windows. Nor were any flowers in evidence as they were in this front room.

'Do you think it was wrong of me to have pushed Michael out to Nightingale Manor?' asked Rachel.

I hesitated. 'Of course not.'

She was gazing at me, agile-eyed, her mouth a little open. She wore no lipstick. She had no make-up on at all and she hadn't bothered to brush her hair. Now she was waiting for me to say more, to elaborate, to reassure her. She sat before me like one accused and I the Judge. A cliché lodged on my tongue: 'I'm sure he found peace there,' I announced.

It was so quiet in this room. I could hear a clock ticking. In all my previous visits I had not been ushered into the front room. I was looking down at my shoes, avoiding Rachel's continuing steady gaze. I became aware of the Persian carpet, the pattern in it.

'I did find it difficult towards the close. But I was hoping for Michael's cure at Nightingale Manor. Mind you, they were very considerate there.'

'I'm sure,' I said, feeling inadequate as I sat there tidily on the sofa.

At last I was relieved to find that she had looked away. I was no longer being closely examined.

'You know I was fond of Michael,' I said. 'I admired him, held him in great esteem. He was a rare human being.'

I was being more or less sincere as I continued my peroration in praise of her husband. No doubt I sounded as if I were giving a funeral oration where only the most blessed and favourable character traits of the dead lamented person are referred to; but I did genuinely warm to Michael Butler, his sense of humour, his courage, his erudition. I would miss him.

A door opened somewhere and briefly I heard the laughter and shouts of children before the door closed again.

'And Michael respected you,' Rachel Butler said.

After another perfunctory silence I announced that I had to leave, that she, Rachel, should come and see me any time at all if she had worries that she thought I could alleviate.

'Just a moment,' she said, 'I nearly forgot. I have something to give you. It's in the other room – something Michael asked me to give you.'

While she was absent I rose from the sofa. Even in this front room there were multiple bookshelves. I examined the photographs on the mantelpiece – one of Michael and his wife together, both looking vulnerably young. I plucked a book out of the shelves and flicked through the pages. Someone, presumably Michael, had marked a cross in the margin opposite lines that he had underlined:

There is nothing too small, but my tenderness paints
it large on a background of gold...
And I thought of Yvonne. I turned the pages back to the title
page. *The Book of Hours* by Rainer Maria Rilke. On the flyleaf
'To Michael with perdurable love, your Rachel. Xmas 1947.'
As Rachel opened the door I slipped the slim volume back
onto the shelf and turned to face her. She was carrying an
envelope. She was holding out the envelope to me like an
offering, like a holy offering, but I recognised the parsimonious
writing on the envelope and I did not wish to take it from her.
Jesus! So it was Michael.
'Michael asked me to give you this,' Rachel Butler said, 'the
last time I was at Nightingale Manor. I mean when Michael was
alive, he asked me to pass this letter on to you after he...after
he...'
'Yes,' I blurted out. 'Thank you.'
I put the envelope into my pocket. I think Rachel hoped I
would open it in front of her, maybe read out its sweet contents.
Naturally she must have been curious.
'Thank you again,' I said unnecessarily.
Bloody hell! That crazy abuse, those threats – and I had
imagined he liked me. 'And Michael respected you,' his widow had
just said. Rachel was talking about her daughters, what a comfort
they were to her and I was remembering how he had written, 'You
are the source of my disgust. Perish your mind. Paralyse your feet.'
He must have been mad, utterly mad. I thought I knew him. We
don't know anybody. Perplexed, we don't even know ourselves –
especially ourselves. I was and am shaken.
In the gloomy passageway that led to the front door, one of the
small grandchildren appeared, clutched at Rachel Butler,
demanding her attention. 'Grandma, grandma, can I have
another butterscotch?'
'In a minute, dear.'
Then, opening the front door for me, she confided discreetly,
'Michael was always so grateful for all the attention you gave

him, doctor. He and I will never forget... I mean I shall never forget your kindness.'

'Grandma, grandma. *Please.*'

I drove away into Belsize Park Avenue before parking the car again. I took the envelope out of my pocket wondering whether this last message from him would deliver to me some apology or an explanation. Or would further abuse be hurled at me and I, again, be cursed? I opened the envelope. It was empty.

April 18th

Again I woke up much too early – before five o'clock. Waking up early I know to be a sign of depression. I could imagine another doctor saying to me, 'Why are you depressed?' And I would answer, 'I'm depressed because I keep waking up too early!' I tried to lie still, eyes closed, but failed to convince myself that a rest was as good as a night's sleep. I kept twisting and turning and mulling over, amongst other things, possible reasons why Michael Butler had sent me those reprehensible, anonymous notes. And, in particular, the symbolic significance of that final empty envelope.

I suppose he resented my power over him. The doctor-patient relationship is necessarily one where the doctor is in a dominating position. The patient lies down on the couch, the doctor examines him standing up. Mentally and physically, the doctor is in the authoritative position. Indeed, if doctor and patient acknowledge each other as equal partners in the sick room the patient would be less confident and less trustful of his physician. Probably he would not, in those circumstances, recover from any transient illness so quickly.

Alas, Michael Butler's ailment was progressive, could not be halted any more than King Canute could stem the tidal waves creeping in further and further. Michael knew it. Inwardly, he must have raged. Angry, too, to be subservient, weak, dependent on me to relieve the tyranny of his pain.

Despite his jocular manner, he needed to assert himself, to challenge my superiority. Bring me down from my pedestal. Those stories, culled from esoteric sources, that he enjoyed telling me, were but one way to raise himself up; by airing his superior erudition he could reveal my relative ignorance. Another way to elevate himself, perhaps was to send me those anonymous notes. In that, he was godlike, a manipulative god whose name should not be uttered, an anonymous god and I, his victim, vulnerable and named. No longer passive, he was God, the great, all-powerful, active practical joker whose face could not be seen, even by a Moses.

Edith came in late this morning. As she took off her overcoat she said, 'Did you hear the news?' I thought she was going to tell me about the house next door. I had already noticed in their front garden a FOR SALE sign – but no, Edith said portentously, 'It was announced on the Home Service this morning that Princess Elizabeth is expecting a second baby next August. I'm so pleased for her.'

Edith takes a close interest in all the gossip about the Royal family. She has a friend who has a friend who works for a Mrs Bassett. That lady had been invited to a Royal Garden Party at Buckingham Palace and reported that in the rear of the park-like gardens was a small lake with ducks and flamingoes! Moreover Mrs Bassett had swiped a few daisies from the royal lawn and now keeps them between the leaves of a book.

'Which particular book?' I had teasingly asked Edith. 'The Bible? P.G. Wodehouse?'

Edith, serious, had replied. 'I'll find out.' And I had glanced at her to see if she was joking. She was not.

That house next door. I wonder whether the floors there are like ours here – not exactly level so that the doors swing back to shut themselves. These big heavy houses in Hampstead have settled into the clay matrix which, according to the degree of rainfall, swells up from to time. Then, sometimes, for a while, we have difficulty in closing the doors at all.

I wonder why Ted Norton is moving. The only occasion I've had a really long conversation with him was when he, rather lachrymose, the New Year's Eve before last, told me about how his old father had become an alcoholic. 'Too many GPs,' Ted had complained, 'think of alcoholics as criminal delinquents rather than patients desperately ill.'

He was right, I suppose. I tend to refer alcoholics for treatment only if they are suffering from such physical complications as polyneuritis or delirium tremens. Maybe I should think of Skid Row as an open-air sick ward without nurses, without doctors.

I can't imagine moving from this house, though it's absurdly grand for only one person to inhabit. The ground floor with its lofty, spacious kitchen, is taken up largely by my waiting and consulting rooms; but I occupy only two of the five rooms upstairs – my bedroom and my study. (Why am I writing all this? Who am I addressing?) I used to tell myself that one day I might need space for a wife and kids. I realise now that will never happen. Still, I would not dare to move – to leave, above all, my mother's master-bedroom. I know it's against godlike reason but I would feel censured. Ridiculously, I think that if a stranger slept in that bedroom it would signal a small treason on my part and I would have to endure all kinds of malefactions.

That room, unused, continues to have my mother's clothes and things untouched in the wardrobe and chests of drawers. It is the pith and marrow of this house even now. Edith ensures that it is hoovered and the windows opened from time to time but I rarely go into it. Last time I entered my mother's bedroom the curtains had not been drawn and the enchantment of a little moonlight crept in. In the algebra of memory there was something missing, one side of the equation. Perhaps it was my father. After all I was born in that room. I fled. In the dark it smelt of mothballs.

I'm sorry Ted Norton will be moving from next door. Let all birds fly, I'll stay here.

April 23rd

I can't remember what it was that Rhys said which stupidly led me to confess to him that I felt irrationally hostile to one of my patients and how much this troubled me.

'For a start,' I said, 'I find his physical appearance repellent.'

I met Rhys's penetrative stare. My own features were being ostentatiously scrutinised. So I added quickly, 'I know what I look like.'

'Ah, the forgery of mirrors,' Rhys sighed, looking into the distance. Then he asked, 'What's the name of your patient?'

Because I didn't see any point in naming Bloomberg, Rhys held forth about how all doctors were as discreet as spies! 'Anyhow,' he added, annoying me, 'I bet the patient you find repellent is Jewish.'

'Why do you say that?'

'Because however much you struggle against it, you're an anti-semite.'

'Rubbish. You've suggested that before. Tosh. I've told you that's not true. Absolutely not so. On what basis . . . ?'

'All right, all right, what are you shouting for? Don't worry about it,' said Rhys pompously. 'Leave self-hatred to the saints.'

His remarks irritated me so much that I forgot to move my queen when it was threatened by his bishop. 'Have it back,' Rhys insincerely persuaded me. Long ago we agreed to abide strictly by the rules. I resigned.

After tea we elected to walk together to the travelling fair which visits the top of the Heath this time of the year. 'Let's have a dekko,' Rhys had suggested. I was glad to have his company. These days he seems to be camped out most of the time in

149

Richmond. I did not know, of course, that we would soon quarrel again. (As I write this I regret it.)

'You know,' Rhys said, when we approached the entrance to Flask Walk, 'in the past I've always had, initially anyway, an exaggerated view of the women I've taken out.'

'Yes,' I agreed, interrupting him, 'they've always been as attractive as Joan Fontaine or Rita Hayworth or...'

'Well, when I knew them better, I've always discovered how ordinary they were. Brummagem gold. With Amy, it's the opposite. The more I come to know her the more extraordinary I discover her to be.'

'She's well?' I asked.

'She's OK.' Rhys bent down to do up a loose shoelace. When he rose he said, 'You know Princess Elizabeth is going to have another baby?'

'Yes.'

'Well, when she read about that in the paper Amy began to weep. And weep. Torrents.'

I don't know why I suddenly felt embarrassed. Some comment was obviously expected of me. But I didn't want to have anything to do with Amy Middleton. I didn't even want to talk about her. So to deflect the direction of our conversation I said – almost at once I regretted it – 'I do know one beautiful woman.'

'What? Who?'

'Yvonne Bloomberg. Anton Bloomberg's young wife.'

'Oh. Do you mean Yvonne Roberts who used to go into the Cosmo sometimes? Didn't know you knew her. Now there's a good example of what I mean. That girl looks as if she's escaped from Paradise but if you chat to her long enough you come to realise she's just very ordinary.'

'Do you think so?' I stammered. 'I don't think so.'

Rhys laughed. 'What are you going so red for?' We were at the top of Heath Street and could hear the music of the fair, carousel music. Rhys advised me, 'Worship her from afar, Robbie. Keep it that way. Perfection is always distant.'

'As far as Richmond,' I said, annoyed.

Rhys laughed again, this time more harshly. 'Amy Middleton's a whore,' I said. 'You give me advice. Let me give you advice. Leave that slut alone. She's trouble, big...'

Rhys just walked away without saying goodbye. So it seems we've quarrelled again. Probably my fault. Lack of sleep makes me irritable and evidently I irritated Rhys. (Before I go to bed tonight I shall take some Nembutal.)

I strolled on and soon found myself amidst a crowd – parents with their excited kids licking toffee apples. I stopped near a man standing on a substantial box. He looked like a beat-up ex-boxer. He stood in front of a caravan blatant with splashes of alarming red and yellow, the colours of schizophrenia. On the caravan in large letters: MADAME ZED, THE GREATEST CLAIR-VOYANT SINCE CASSANDRA.

'Those of you who were here last week,' the burly man shouted hoarsely, 'heard what pagan Madame Zed prophesied. That a stork would fly over Buckingham Palace. Wasn't she right? And last Monday, ladies and gentlemen, didn't Madame Zed say what would be in the budget – that the chancellor would raise the price of petrol?'

'I could have told you that,' someone in the crowd yelled.

'By nine pence a gallon? That it would be three bob a gallon, didja fathom that out, sir?'

The rough advocate for Madame Zed continued to extol her clairvoyant abilities and to wave his arms. I thought how people gesticulate strenuously when they don't believe in the strength of the words they are uttering. Then I came home.

I can't write down any more tonight. It has been a miserable day. I'm tired. And I'm sick of talking to myself.

April 26th

On returning from my afternoon rounds I spied Pickford's giant van outside the next door house, and over the hedge men were threading their way through the front garden carrying furniture. Ted Norton, who has been my neighbour for the last three years, seemed to be supervising them. I spoke briefly to Ted. He is a physicist and he is shifting his family to near Aldermaston where he has a new job.

I wonder how much he is asking for his property. I didn't like to ask. I guessed Edith would find out.

'How long have you lived in your house?' queried Ted Norton. 'Oh, forever,' I replied.

Later, when Edith brought in my tea on a tray, she said excitedly, 'Do you know what the Nortons want for their house? £4500. Crikey. They can ask but they won't get. That next door house is going to be empty for a long time.'

Forever, I had said. It was true; it was my forever. I was born in this house. For years before the war, when I was a schoolboy, we had the Mills family as our neighbours. Ron Mills was a year older than me. Bluebells. One late April we had cycled out into the country to pick bluebells for our mothers. Beyond Barnet, some-where in the vicinity of Hadley Woods, we had to pass under a railway bridge - more a tunnel than a bridge – and it owned, we discovered, a fantastic acoustic echo. We alighted from our bikes and shouted to hear our voices return and return and return until they faded.

Ron said, 'You told me you were an atheist, right? So shout out in this tunnel that you don't believe in God. Go on.' I didn't really feel like yelling out the substance of what I called at that time, 'my credo'. Ron Mills was insistent.

'You're scared,' he taunted me. 'I don't think you're a sincere atheist.'

'I am,' I insisted. 'Religion is all superstition and I'm not superstitious. I always walk under ladders.'

Ron Mills stood beside his bike challenging me, daring me to tell God that I didn't believe in him and so, as a consequence of 'a boy's honour' I had finally to shout out, 'I don't believe in God.' And the echo of an echo of an echo returned my cry, 'In God...in God...in God.'

I hear it still and I remember my sudden fear when, as we were mounting our bikes, the tunnel rumbled angrily as if God had taken umbrage. Several seconds passed before we both realised a train was passing over.

Ron Mills, apart from talking to me about the mystery of the universe, referred frequently to the mystery of girls. He reckoned, ridiculously, that they liked their breasts to be touched. 'An' if you stick your tongue in their ear, they go wild,' he assured me.

'I wouldn't fancy doing that,' I had said; but for years I would day-dream of sticking my tongue into my Liverpool cousin's ear.

April 29th

Though the Bloombergs' spacious sitting room was far from being crowded, I was pressed back against a radiator by a fast-talking, thin, nervous lady with bulging eyes. I felt the heat at my back and I thought how Edith would approve of this *centrally-heated*, modern apartment with its fitted carpets. And Rhys would have described the busy lady facing me as a mixture of Bette Davis and Pop-eye's wife.

Over her shoulder, through the standing figures, I saw Anton Bloomberg, morose, glass in hand, conferring with Hugh Fisher as they reclined on a large, over-cushioned sofa. Of the other dozen or so guests, I only knew Mrs Levy. Yvonne, I believed, was in the kitchen, preparing the food.

'I agree with Herbert Read,' the lady talking at me continued, 'Nash is essentially a water colourist even when he paints in oils but David . . . '

Five minutes earlier I had been attracted to a framed flame of a painting on the white wall, which had been hung to the right of the windows close to the *toile de joie* curtains.

'Do you like it?' the exophthalmic intense lady said, who, friendly, unsolicited, had joined me. 'It's by Bomberg.'

'I didn't know he had such talent,' I replied, mishearing her –
believing she had said Bloomberg not Bomberg.

'David is much neglected,' my new friend agreed.

'David?'

'David Bomberg. I happen to know him. That's why I feel free
to call him David.'

'Oh yes. David Bomberg,' I repeated.

I looked at the so-called Cornish landscape again. The strong,
thick, broad brush strokes, oblique and horizontal, of browns,
yellows and orange suggested an African or Middle Eastern
desert rather than a pastoral, Cornish scene.

'David is bitter that he isn't more prized by the Art
establishment.'

'Jewish paranoia?'

'I don't think so.' She glared at me as if I had made an anti-
semitic remark.

When we were called into the kitchen to eat at a huge, long
table fit for a royal feast, I managed to escape from the friend of
David Bomberg. I sat next to Mrs Levy and someone who
introduced himself as Ben Moore. He, too, was a leading light at
the Broadhurst Gardens Centre and one whom I discovered had
political ambitions.

During our meal I observed Bloomberg at the head of the table
filling up his own wine glass again and again. He looked sullen.
I guessed he wished he was with his pianist, elsewhere. Yvonne
also appeared to be less than happy, forcing smiles I thought, as
she went in and out of the kitchen and attended to guests. Hugh
Fisher was helping her, as if he were the host, not Anton
Bloomberg.

Ben Moore held forth about the danger of a monstrous clash
between the Great Powers – Soviet Russia and the USA. 'In a
year, or a decade, or a century hence, sooner or later all of
Europe will be reduced to rubble. And the survivors, thrashing
around in a radioactive wilderness, will descend into
unimaginable barbarism!'

'We know all about unimaginable barbarism already,' Mrs Levy interjected.

I thought of the rainbow I had seen from the garden door but Mrs Levy was relating another version of God's promise to man, how God, intending to destroy the wicked cities of Sodom and Gomorrah had been begged by the angels to reconsider His decision since there may be thirty-six just men living in those places.

'As long as there are thirty-six just men in the world God will spare us all,' Mrs Levy argued with some confidence.

'What about the women?' Hugh Fisher asked. 'Are there no just women?'

'In Jewish legend women don't count,' Ben Moore replied.

I wondered how much Hugh Fisher had Yvonne in mind. Afterwards, when most of the guests had returned to the large sitting room, I joined Yvonne and Fisher in the kitchen to help with the washing up. Anton Bloomberg was drinking heavily next door and I was in the presence of a woman, surely one of the Just, with whom I had a noble and chaste friendship, one unsullied by adultery with its concomitant deceptions and secretiveness. As for Hugh Fisher, he smiled at me in millimetres.

Before we had finished cleaning up, Anton Bloomberg came into the kitchen and said thickly to me, 'Can I have a word with you?' I saw Fisher staring at us both wonderingly. I followed Bloomberg out of the kitchen down a passageway into an intimate, book-heavy study. He turned and reversed unsteadily, coming close to me. To claim my personal space I sat down quickly into an amber-coloured chair and he collapsed into one too, before clumsily drawing it nearer to me!

'I'm not drunk,' he insisted.

I could see the gramophone, stacks of records and, on his desk, next to a typewriter, a ginger cat, curled up like the capital letter C, asleep.

'Ah yes, the damned cat. Great for my asthma, right? I've given her everything,' he grumbled. 'She didn't like the dog so I got rid of the dog. She wanted a cat so I let her keep the cat. I wheeze as a result. I'm allergic to the damned thing. She wants Hugh Fisher to leave the BBC and work for us and I've said Yes. I've always said Yes. Yes Yes Yes I've said. Now all she can say is No.'

He stood up, swayed a little, shook his head negatively, sadly, then sat down again.

'And I've left her alone as you recommended. It didn't work.'

'You found... consolation elsewhere?'

Bloomberg focused his eyes on me, a threatening aspect to his features as happens sometimes when a drunk feels challenged. Then his face melted into benignity.

'Yes,' he admitted. 'I had a relationship with an Israeli musician. Yvonne knew all about it. I told her.'

'You told her?'

'It's all over now,' Bloomberg said forlornly. 'Over now.'

I could see the Adam's apple in his throat moving up and down as he swallowed whatever saliva he had in his mouth.

'Speak to Yvonne,' Bloomberg said louder, commanding me. 'Speak to her. She respects you. She's taken a shine to you. Please speak to her.'

He brought his fist down hard on the desk and the ginger cat, startled, raised its head.

'Some time, somewhere else,' I said, 'I'll talk to her.' I twisted my wrist round so that I could read my watch. 'I must go home soon.'

We returned down the passageway. Wedlock, I thought, with the emphasis on 'lock'. Bloomberg, more composed, side-stepped into the kitchen and I advanced towards the noise of the main party. Ben Moore, as if on a platform, was addressing half a dozen people including David Bomberg's friend. She lit a cigarette and I noticed how her fingers trembled perceptibly. Her thinness, her nervous energy, her exophthalmos, her trembling fingers, added up to the spot-diagnosis of thyrotoxicosis.

When I was a medical student, I read in one of my textbooks

a case history I have never forgotten. A woman was cycling through a dark tunnel at night – perhaps it was similar to the one near Hadley Wood where I once shouted out, 'I don't believe in God' – when suddenly she heard the noise of a motor car behind her, then her moving shadow was thrown on to the walls of the tunnel by the oncoming headlights. In a panic, she cycled faster and faster and, eyes wide, she glanced backwards. The dazzling headlights blinded her. The woman began to scream with fright as, desperate, she pedalled on even more rapidly. Cyclist and automobile emerged from the tunnel simultaneously. The motor car raced on, its blood-red tail-lights disappearing behind a far curved hedge. The woman stood beside her bicycle at the roadside, her heart beating fast and her hands trembling. As time passed her heartbeat did not resume its normal rate. If it went on beating with such rapidity, untreated, she would die of heart failure. When she visited a doctor he found that her thyroid gland in her neck had become enlarged. She had cycled into the tunnel essentially healthy; she had come out the other side suffering from thyrotoxicosis.

I could hear Ben Moore boom, 'Stalin has agreed to assist Mao Tse-tung. So you *should* be worried, Colin. He's pledged three hundred million dollars in aid...'

Yvonne came into the room and it was all light. She was followed by Hugh Fisher. Had Anton Bloomberg retired to his study? Each time I look at Yvonne her loveliness startles and delights me. Neither Isolde nor Helen of Troy had her importance of beauty. She and Hugh Fisher carried in trays of cups and a large cake with thirty candles on it.

I doodled the next half hour away, talking to Mrs Levy and to a man who, in the afternoon, had been to Wembley to watch the Cup Final. Arsenal had beaten Liverpool 2–0. I heard the ghost of Michael Butler applaud. Mrs Levy told me how much she looked forward to my talk on 'The New Frontiers of Medicine' and then we sang 'Happy Birthday, Hugh,' before he blew out the candles. I watched Yvonne, the grace of her arms, the

ABSE

tastefulness of her turquoise dress, which showed off her slim waist rising and flowering into the fullness of her breasts.

When I took my leave Yvonne accompanied me to the lift. Hesitating, she said quietly, 'I'm in trouble, Robbie.' I was close to her, aware of her perfume. And I said, touching her bare arm gently, 'Then come and see me at my surgery.'

May 5th

All this week, each day, I have opened the door of my waiting room to call in the next patient, hoping to discover Yvonne there. Why hasn't she come? Is it because she does not wish our relationship to become impersonal – that of doctor and patient? In the ambience of a physician's surgery the most intimate concerns of the patient can be discussed. The doctor, listening, may exhibit his sympathy but not his profound love. The doctor, under clinical circumstances, has to keep his distance, act with propriety. Maybe Yvonne realises this – would prefer to consult me as a friend rather than as a doctor? Alas, as a doctor I can do little; as a friend I can do less. At least I, being a doctor, have some sanction to confront her husband. But what action should I take should she come? Are there not occasions and honesties when it is just to submit to the holiness of the god, Dionysus, and to act with evil intent out of pure altruism?

Before my evening surgery, while I was at my desk, Edith entered with two vases of fresh lilac which she had cut from the tree in the garden. She chatted away as usual.

'Your mother would have been proud of you,' she postulated. 'I've read that leaflet on your desk. The most respected General Practitioner in North London ... '

The leaflet had irritated me. Not only did it spell my name wrongly – Dr Robert Symonds – but, in promoting my talk 'The New Frontiers of Medicine', whoever had written the blurb had

158

gone over the top. Theoretically, it could even get me into trouble with the General Medical Council. They are very strict these days about doctors advertising their skills. Still, I was not responsible for that blurb.

I don't know why the GMC should be so fussy about doctors advertising their degrees and skills (too vulgar?) when they are so gentlemanly when it comes to more serious transgressions. There are many doctors, eyes glinting like scalpels dangerously, who should be struck off the Register because of their incompetence or ignorance. Some practising not too far from Hampstead still prescribe barbarous pre-antibiotic remedies and, if something goes wrong, they know they can rely on the efficient Medical Defence Union to help them out. The medical profession closes its ranks when a physician immoderately blunders. If I did not keep up-to-date I would be too disgusted by my own ignorance and ineptitude. I would not be able to live with myself.

I'd only been half listening to Edith but now her remarks caught my attention. 'Wouldn't it be extraordinary if your father came back from Canada and bought the house next door?' she conjectured.

Indeed it would be extraordinary. I don't even know if he is alive. He has never tried to get in touch with me. He would be in his late seventies if he still survives; as far as I am concerned, he can go to hell – if he isn't there already.

'People go to Canada,' Edith fantasised, 'people go to Australia and some come back millionaires. You might have one photograph of him on view somewhere in the house. Just in case.'

After Edith went out I thought of how my father abandoned my mother. The cruelty of it. And her ridiculous, perdurable concern for him. The cruelty of devotion! And how later, she had developed tuberculosis and had died just before the antibiotic revolution, before Waksman and his co-workers at Rutgers University, Albert Schatz and Elizabeth Bugie, had discovered streptomycin. If she had only hung on a little longer.

If only some researcher earlier than Waksman had thought about why the tubercle bacillus did not thrive in the earth – that there was something in the soil that could combat tuberculosis. After all, the soil as a form of medicine had an age-old tradition. Shouldn't we have taken notice that our pet animals eat the good earth from time to time? Besides, the widespread custom of earth-eating was not only religious but partly medicinal. The ancient Egyptians recommended soil-eating in their papyri. The Otomac Indians, I read somewhere, ate a fine, yellowish, greasy clay; and is it not written in Ecclesiastes, 'The Lord hath created medicines out of the earth: and he that is wise will not abhor them'? Waksman looked to the earth and delivered us streptomycin.

But now, as I write all this, I breathe in another gift of the earth, the faint scent of the lilac that Edith has arranged in these two vases, and my mind goes blank.

May 7th

A scrum of people, including Ben Moore, survivors from the Annual General Meeting, were already gathered in the institution-like foyer of the Broadhurst Gardens Centre when I arrived. A woman I had not seen before sat behind a white-clothed table taking the small entrance fee to cover the cost of the tea and biscuits after my lecture. I overheard Ben Moore's cannon of a voice boom, 'In this era of austerity isn't it appropriate that Attlee is in charge rather than a colourful Winston Churchill or a robust Aneurin Bevan?'

Mrs Levy was at my elbow. 'I'm to lead you to what we call our green room.'

In that modest ante-room Hugh Fisher awaited me, more nervous apparently than I was. He had looked up my entry in the current *Medical Directory* and had noted that in 1938 I had contributed an essay on 'Painting and Science' to *Art Quarterly* and that in 1939 a monograph by me entitled 'The White Plague

– Tuberculosis, Then and Now' had been published in *The Medicaster*.

'Is there any other publication I should refer to?' asked Hugh Fisher. 'Didn't you publish something about euthanasia?'

'No,' I said. 'I've only published twice in my life.'

'I hope you agree to take questions afterwards.'

Mrs Levy, who had joined us, recounted how she had attended a talk at her synagogue hall where questions also had been called for. 'Nobody moved a muscle,' said Mrs Levy. 'Silence for half a minute. Then a woman put up her hand and asked, "Please, where's the toilet?"'

Hugh Fisher did not laugh. He, preoccupied, kept glancing at a piece of paper on which he had written his opening remarks.

Mrs Levy, more relaxed, reassured me that because posters announcing my lecture, 'The New Frontiers of Medicine', had been slapped on half the walls and trees of Hampstead and because NW3 was inhabited by hypochondriacs, I would have a reasonable-sized audience. 'Your own patients, for a start, should turn up,' she pondered.

I wanted to refer quietly to my own notes, I wanted to appear sensible in front of an audience that would include Yvonne but Mrs Levy was in full flow. She was suggesting that because I was the man of the moment I shouldn't get big-headed. 'You know the Chassidic story of Rabbi Shmelke, the wise, celebrated Shmelke of Nikolsburg?'

'No,' I said.

'When he came to be honoured, to listen to speeches in praise of him, he asked to go into a room like this, one with a mirror. He then stood in front of his reflection and addressed it. "You are wonderful, Rabbi Shmelke," Shmelke said, "generous, compassionate, a paragon of virtue, peerless and flawless." The others in the room were disturbed by this self-praise. Then Shmelke said, "Having uttered these absurdities I am now ready to listen to your flattery."'

While Hugh Fisher adjusted the microphone and introduced

me I examined the audience. To my astonishment I observed Rhys sitting near the front. Only when Hugh Fisher sat down and I advanced to the microphone did I see Yvonne. She was wearing dark spectacles, dark sunglasses indoors. Why? The audience had stopped clapping. Had Bloomberg, the swine, given her a black eye? I was aware of silence. They were waiting for me to begin.

Three-quarters of an hour later, it was time to conclude my lecture. I had dwelt on the onset and development of the antibiotic revolution concluding with reference to the new typhoid-fever defying drug, chloramphenicol. 'It has been used,' I said, 'to combat all kinds of minor infections, from earache to tonsillitis, from septic cuts to whooping cough, as well as to combat typhoid fever for which it is specific. I've prescribed it frequently myself. But now it is being reported that it can damage the bone marrow and cause serious blood disorders. It is not an antibiotic I shall now hurry to prescribe. Even as one dark door creaks back for the first time, the research doctor with his probing torch comes upon another dark, beckoning passage-way...' I hesitated, became aware of Rhys grinning up at me, presumably because of my rhetoric. 'Beckoning passageway,' I repeated, referring to my notes, 'to yet another locked door behind which lies yet another dark labyrinth, another mystery.' I sat down to applause but could not help scrutinising Rhys's mocking face.

Lanky Hugh Fisher, kangaroo-like, bounded to the micro-phone and announced, 'Dr Simmonds has kindly offered to answer any of your questions.' A suspenseful silence followed and I thought of Mrs Levy's toilet-seeking lady. At last, someone asked, 'When are doctors going to find the cure for the common cold?' Subsequently others put up their hands and I tried to respond to their questions.

Then I heard the booming voice of Ben Moore. 'In the chairman's introduction we learnt that you are an expert on Art's effect upon Science. Could you...'

'It's the other way round,' I interrupted. 'For instance, in paintings of the crucifixion before William Harvey discovered the circulation of the blood in 1628, the wound in Jesus's chest was almost invariably depicted on the right, not where the heart is on the left. Later artists knew better.'

'And with that interesting piece of information,' Hugh Fisher said, 'it's time for us all to be refreshed with a cup of tea.'

Soon after I came down the wooden steps from the platform I was disappointed to see Yvonne disappearing through the front exit door. I was collared by one of my patients, a Mrs Harvey. 'Didn't you prescribe chloram-whatever-you-call-it for me once, doctor?' Finally, I was rescued by Rhys. 'How about our Sunday game of chess?' he said, as if we had never had that silly small quarrel.

May 8th

Before we played markedly aggressive chess yesterday evening, I happened to remark how delighted I was that he, Rhys, had taken the trouble to come to my lecture. From his reaction I discerned again the ambivalence of his feelings towards me. I had not expected him to be smarmy about my performance at Broadhurst Gardens but there is nothing reprehensible in exaggerating the truth a little to please a friend.

Instead, he did not refer to my lecture at all directly. He simply let me know that the gap-toothed lady sitting next to him fell asleep during my performance and that, even as he rose from his chair, she had stayed behind in seemingly permanent undisturbable sloth. He reassured me, 'Trying to impress that cosy catarrhal audience, Robbie, is like letting off a squib during the Blitz. I'm glad I didn't bring Amy along.'

Envy holds a dagger.

When Jason Fowler's twin brother was discovered to be a diabetic, Jason worried whether he, too, had the misfortune to be dogged by diabetes. He had no symptoms – nevertheless I had asked him to bring along a sample of his urine to the surgery. This he did this morning.

I mixed a few cc. of the urine with an equal quantity of Fehling's solution, then held the test-tube over the bunsen burner for a few minutes. No yellow or red precipitate became visible. No sugar in the urine. I was able to bury his fears. It is a sacred privilege to be the bearer of good news, to tell a patient, who perhaps has dreamt of worms and epitaphs for some time, that his anxieties are needless; to speak with sincerity and gentle order, quietly, without trumpets, without drums, 'You are well.' And to receive the expressed gratitude of the patient as if, godlike, omniscient, one has bequeathed him or her the benediction of true health. Jason Fowler came into my consulting room this morning sombre-faced; he left smiling.

Jason Fowler was the last patient of the morning and after he'd gone I thought of a particular long afternoon at Westminster Hospital years ago when I was a fourth year medical student. The registrar had decided to teach us a singularly important principle of medicine. He asked a nurse to fetch him a sample of urine. He then talked to us about diabetes mellitus. '*Diabetes*,' he said, 'is a Greek name; but the Romans noticed that bees liked the urine of diabetics so they added the word *mellitus* which means sweet as honey. Well, as you know, you may find sugar in the urine of a diabetic ... '

By now the nurse had returned with a sample of urine which the registrar promptly held up like a trophy. We stared at that straw-coloured fluid as if we had never seen such a thing before. The registrar then startled us. He dipped a finger boldly in the urine then licked that finger with the tip of his tongue. As if tasting a delicious vintage of wine he opened and closed his lips rapidly. Could he perhaps detect a faint taste of sugar? The sample was passed on to us for an opinion. We all dipped a finger into the fluid, all of us foolishly licked that finger.

'Now,' said the registrar, 'you have learnt the first principle of diagnosis. I mean the power of observation. You see I dipped my *middle* finger into the urine but licked my index finger – not like you chaps.'

He laughed. We did not. 'Big deal,' Charlie Forster whispered to me as the registrar continued to laugh and the nurse smiled broadly.

That was a peculiar time: the fourth year of my medical studies, my first year of clinical experience. I remember how I deliberately omitted to tell my mother about my pathetic confrontation with my first patient. That same registrar had detailed me to take the case history of a patient in Cubicle D. I pulled aside the orange-brown curtains (I can see them vividly as I write) to discover a man of about 35 staring intently at the electric bulb above him. To my polite, 'Good morning,' he said. 'See that bulb?'

'Yes.'

'That is Destiny.'

Somewhat disconcerted, I tried uselessly to elicit a case history. He ignored my fumbling questions and eventually he shouted, 'Get me Cunningham 2961.'

'What?'

'Phone 2961.'

I did not know what to do. This was beyond the limits of the ordinary. He continued to stare with his very blue eyes at the electric bulb and rambled on about the Judgement Book, Heaven's pornography. Then, at last, he turned his head to observe me for the first time. 'Never apologise for your victories,' he said. 'Are you phoning Cunningham 2961?'

I thought it best to humour him. 'I've tried,' I said. 'The number's engaged.'

'Try again,' he commanded me and turned again to stare at the electric bulb. 'Then come over here and feel my penis.'

I slipped quickly out of the cubicle and caught up with the registrar.

May 9th
She came at last. She was still wearing dark glasses and her hair-style seemed changed. When I asked Yvonne why she had rushed off on Sunday evening, she confessed, 'I didn't want you to see me in such a state. I desperately wanted to hear you lecture so I came. Oh Robbie ...I'm hardly a picture now but my need to ask you to help me overrides my vanity. Who else can I ask, if not you?'

She lifted off her spectacles. With them on I would have agreed with Rhys – she looked like a Hollywood film star; shorn of them, undisguised, she resembled one of those sacred faces, one of those angels depicted in Renaissance paintings, but one brutally vandalised: her left eye half-closed, the side of her face – partially hidden by her hair – bruised into hatched colours and rudely swollen.

'He's a monster,' I exclaimed.

When Yvonne so tentatively asked if I remembered the novel she had once given me about Dr Glas, for a moment I held my breath.

'He poisoned the husband with cyanide,' I said.

'Oh no, no. For heaven's sake, Robbie. No, I mean at the beginning of the novel. Dr Glas warns his patient not to make love ... because of his heart ... there's nothing wrong with Anton's heart. But he's troubled by his asthma, especially lately.'

It was bold of her, considering her innate modesty, to suggest indirectly that I should prescribe something for Bloomberg's asthma that would also radically subdue his rampant sexual aggression.

'To reduce it anyway,' Yvonne almost whispered. 'You gave him bromides once, remember?' She avoided my gaze, looked down at the floor like one ashamed.

'You're married,' I said. 'You must expect to be made love to.'

'I do. I know my duty. I mean I expect to... sometimes. But Anton's wild... and his sexual energy seems limitless. More than ever I find his physical presence intolerable. Even so... if he'd only...'

She raised her bowed head, looked at me appealingly – her face like a silent cry for help.

Who am I to judge her? What am I if not a friend, a constant friend?

'You should seek a divorce,' I said.

Yvonne began to weep and I rose from my chair to comfort her. I could have been living not in this surgery with its weighing machine, its test-tubes for urine in a rack, its safe medicine chest, my desk, the flowers Edith always arranges in vases – but in a novel, a Swedish novel published in 1905. I could have been wearing Dr Glas's shoes, his very clothes, when I promised her, 'I'll think of something.'

She managed to control herself. She extracted a small handkerchief from her handbag, wiped away tears from her bruised cheek. 'I'm sorry,' she said.

I rose, moved towards her and rested my hand gently on her head. I stroked her hair as one might a child's. An affectionate gesture. For a few seconds I permitted myself to remain very close to her – me standing up, she sitting there. I inhaled her faint perfume before I broke away.

'Anton says that I am afraid of sex, that I'm worried about having a baby because of what happened to my mother. That's nonsense. Such is his pride he can't realise it's he whom I flinch from.'

I wanted to take her in my arms and soothe her, to feel her breasts' responsive pressure, no more than that. Instead I had only touched her head lightly. That was permissible.

After Yvonne left my surgery I brooded at my desk for a long time – 'Don't be a fool,' I kept telling myself. 'Remember your oath, the Hippocratic oath – I will follow that system of regimen which according to my ability and judgement I consider for the benefit of my patient and abstain from whatever is deleterious and mischievous.' But what if there are two patients to treat and by benefiting one the regimen is deleterious to the other?

And then it crossed my mind like a shadow, as it had before: was my chaste Yvonne being not helpless but cunning – had she from the start given me that novel purposefully? It cannot be. I reminded myself of how once I had imagined Amy Middleton was attempting to entrap me. 'You don't trust people because of your boyhood Guy Fawkes accident,' Charlie Forster had said.

Certainly, apart from the question of ordinary morality, there is a real danger to myself. I have everything to lose. It would be better that Yvonne should sue for a divorce. She should have her photograph taken while her features are so battered. I would testify to her husband's brutality. All right, they were bound to each other economically. And divorce proceedings take such a long time. Allegations of sadistic conduct would have to be mounted in detail and each trivial incident inflated to operatic proportions.

Poor meek young girl. She should not have got married in the first place – certainly not to a man like Bloomberg. I share her repugnance towards him. But repugnance is not excuse enough for her to outstretch her hand and ward him off night after frustrated night nor for me to be self-destructively rash.

I keep returning in thought to Dr Glas and recall how he had examined his patient's heart, the Reverend Gregorius's heart, knowing there was nothing wrong with it; had examined him at length, deliberately moving his stethoscope across his chest, from below the left clavicle to the apex beat, displaying as he did so, a gravely fake concern. How alarmed his patient must have become! Doubtless more so when Dr Glas blithely announced that sexual congress with his wife could be dangerous – 'A question of your life,' Dr Glas had intoned. 'I find it hard to believe it would be to your taste to drop dead like the late-lamented King Frederick I or more recently M. Felix Faurée...'

Could I translate into reality Dr Glas's fictional so-called heart examination into one more considerate, more benign – and yet achieve a positive result?

I went upstairs to my study to retrieve Söderberg's novel. I wanted to remember the details of that tricky consultation in Dr Glas's office. I found the relevant page and read Dr Glas's entry in his journal: 'I avoided looking at him as I spoke. But when I had made an end, I saw that he was sitting there with his hand over his eyes, and that his lips were moving. And I guessed rather than heard: Our Father, which art in Heaven, hallowed be Thy name... lead us not into temptation, but deliver us from evil...'

Could I, I wonder, the next time I had cause to examine Bloomberg's chest, place my stethoscope here, there, listen adagio, look up, tantalisingly hesitate before pronouncing in solemn tones, 'Anton, your asthma over the years has taken its toll, has, I fear, strained your heart. It's precarious. I'm very worried about your heart.' Then, following an electrocardiogram, advise him urgently to avoid sexual excitement at all costs!

How would Bloomberg react? Would he silently mumble the moaning Jewish equivalent, whatever that might be, of our Lord's prayer? No, he's not that sort of a guy. He would ask me to refer him to a cardiologist for a second opinion.

May 10th

I woke up to early sunlight flooding the bedroom. I had been dreaming of a fire. I remember little, only the departing skirts of the dream. Charlie Forster and I were dissecting the corpse on the slab, muscles all exposed as in the plate of an anatomy manual, the face covered by a cloth. Suddenly the body sat up, the cloth fell away to reveal Anton Bloomberg's face. 'Its senseless eyes are open,' Charlie warned me. 'Achtung, achtung!' We tried to put the body into a wardrobe but when we opened it flames leapt out and everything caught fire, a blinding fire.

That is all I can remember of my dream.

169

From the window I could see the sky's uninterrupted blue above the brick-coloured rooftops. The wind, during the night, had brought down more of the cherry blossom from the trees across the road. It was as if someone had torn up the *Financial Times* leaving its pink fragments in the gutter.

'Its senseless eyes are open,' Charlie had said in my dream. Wasn't that the same phrase Dr Glas had used about his poisoned victim while he wrote out the death certificate... dead of a heart attack. Still wearing my pyjamas I consulted Söderberg's novel in my study and re-read how the Rev. Gregorius had swallowed the pill that Dr Glas had recommended for his indigestion, ignorant, of course, that it was deadly cyanide. Glas pretended to be preoccupied but he witnessed it all. 'He saw his patient's arm fall limply down, his head nod on his chest and *his senseless eyes wide open.*'

This afternoon I finished my rounds early, the fret of it, the language of illness, and parked my Morris Minor near the border of the Heath. I wanted to escape for an hour or two, to breathe in the life-enhancing air of the Heath, to enjoy the stretched silence of a great sunlit space, to forget my patients, my diagnostic dilemmas, my responsibilities, attachments, dreams. As I took the path into the Heath I was dismayed to see the lanky figure of Hugh Fisher ahead of me. I slowed my pace and took a tangential direction. I did not feel convivial.

Soon after, I reclined on the turf under a monarch of a sycamore tree and peered up through its green-leaved, criss-cross branches at the jigsaw of a blue sky. I felt lightened, then sleepy. Perhaps it was the drowsy hum of London's distant, interminable traffic and the birdsong nearby. Was that a nightingale? I remember my mother telling me that nightingales sang during the daytime when they were seeking a mate. I could not whistle up one woman. It would have been good to have shared these moments, numinous moments of lying under the tabernacle of a sycamore tree with some dear companion, with Yvonne.

When I awoke I heard the sound of the sea. It was the rising evening wind sighing in the sycamore. I sat up. For no evident reason my Liverpool uncle came to mind, my mother's brother, Marjorie's father. He was one who did not know the virtue of reticence. 'I fixed it,' he would say and 'He couldn't put it over on me,' and 'So I showed them.' He was devoid of the trained diffidence of most Englishmen who prefer to say, 'One' rather than 'I'. One has had an article published in a learned journal. One gave a lecture on 'New Trends in Medicine'.

It must have been the wind in the sycamore tree with its sound of the sea that made me think of my dead uncle. Mother liked to take our seaside holidays at Salcombe in Devon and one summer our Liverpool relations joined us. After supper one evening I left the rented house and went for a walk, walking on and on aimlessly. I kept going though it began to get dark. Marjorie was allowed to stay out relatively late but I was only thirteen. On my return journey I still lingered on the beach listening to the sea. When I did get back and received a scolding, I heard my uncle say to my mother, 'That boy needs a father.'

Who has not become lyrical or melancholy or philosophical beside the sea? Who has not been consoled by the sound of the waves' irregularities, by the pitch and tone of them, the 'sssh' of shingle, the way the sea slaps on rocks or shuffles into the sand that sizzles as the tide recedes? The 'sssh' in the branches of the sycamore was but a substitute. I listened to it and thought desultorily of my uncle. But soon it would be time for my evening surgery. As bad luck would have it, when I joined the path I saw Hugh Fisher returning from wherever he'd been.

'It was a most engaging talk you gave,' he giggled. 'All the committee thought so too.'

'You're playing truant from the BBC?' I asked.

'Oh no. I've quit the BBC. I'm already working for the Bloombergs. Anton went off yesterday to Sweden. His sister who lived there has just died. He's gone to her funeral.'

'So you're minding the shop?'

He giggled. 'Hardly. Anton will be back next week. He'll

complete some business transactions while he's there. We import
and export quite a lot to and from Sweden, you know.'

Hugh Fisher, in his fussy, ladylike way, proceeded to tell me
in detail and at length the different items the firm imported and
exported. I think I must have gone glassy-eyed. Nevertheless,
when we reached the border of the Heath and my car was in sight
I felt obliged to offer him a lift. One has to be prepared to pay a
high price for a good deed. Fortunately he declined.

'Thanks,' he said, 'but I'm going into Keats Grove. I'm seeing
a man about a map.'

'A map?'

'Yes, I collect old maps. Apart from the pictorial beauty of maps
they help us understand the world we live in, don't you think?'

'I suppose so,' I assented politely, without conviction.

At South End Green, by way of a valediction, he added, self-
deprecatingly, 'Some people become explorers. I collect old
maps.' He waved a hand limply before loping off towards Keats
Grove while I retrieved my car.

I had travelled only some hundred yards when I first heard,
then saw, a bearded man wearing a kilt and playing bagpipes as
he came towards me. He sheared off into the grassy Heath,
marching on, a one-man army, and I thought, 'This is
Hampstead.' I heard myself laugh aloud as I recollected that the
French reckon kilts are a liability in war but good for love.

Bloomberg. What shall I do? What can I do? When he's back
from Sweden, what drugs dare I prescribe that are not too harmful
and yet would infallibly reduce Anton Bloomberg to a eunuch? I
wish I knew more about pharmacology. I wish I knew less.

I once read a book by Kierkegaard (I did not finish it). I
remember how he praised Abraham above all other heroes
because he obeyed God's order to sacrifice his son, Isaac. An
evil command would be obeyed because it originated from on
high. Kierkegaard defined acceptance of such a holy injunction
as the teleological suspension of the ethical. Are evil commands
only legitimate if God-directed?

On my return home, Edith told me the Post Office had delivered a bulky parcel. 'A box, I think. I took it up to your study. It was quite heavy,' she accused me.

I undid the string and the brown paper impatiently. Yes, a box. I opened it up. A chess set – not an ordinary chess set either, but one with delicately carved ivory pieces. The card read: 'Sorry, mate. Forgive me, kiddo. See you Sunday – your ludicrous Rhys.'

God, it must have cost him a bomb. That's Rhys – totally unpredictable.

May 13th

I paid a visit to one of my patients this afternoon: Millie Watts who is 101. Supposing she lived on and on and on? On her 200th birthday would people begin to pray to her as if she were a goddess? She seems fitter than her pessimistic seventy-year-old daughter who looks after her and who always moans about the insolubility of most human dilemmas and the losses and disaffections in modern life. Millie has an ageing son also. He recently moved to a house close to Golders Green Crematorium. When Edith typed the new address on his clinical card she said, 'Very convenient.'

The child asks, 'Why?' The adolescent, 'How?' The adult, 'Where?' And the old, 'When?'

Yet there may be something in the vague philosophical notion that we die only when we are ready for death. I have long believed that we all have a suicide potential varying from very high to very low that is in combat with our strong or weak 'will to live'. Millie's will to live is high. Her suicide potential low. She should go on for years yet.

This afternoon on my rounds, examining Mrs Harvey's niece, I could not help thinking of that doctor I met a couple of years ago at a British Medical Association dinner, a Dr Platt who, smiling, spoke of the pleasurable experiences of medical practice. 'Not

least,' he said, 'the beautiful vision of young women unclothed
to the waist. Visions given to artists and doctors in the course of
their work. It is something which can be quite unrelated to desire
or to sexual arousal. It is like viewing a Tiepolo Venus.'

May 14th
I must recall, as if before a Judge, exactly how it happened. First
the phone waking me up from oblivion. In the darkness its
persistent clamour, like a blunt knife, prodding me to respond. I
leant over to switch on the bedside lamp and though the light
assaulted my eyes I read the figures on the clock. It was just after
3 a.m., the time of the owl. I picked up the receiver and heard the
panic in a man's voice.
  'Anton's asthma has gone on for hours. He's going blueish in
the face.'
  'Who's speaking?'
  'Hugh, Hugh Fisher. He's taken the tablets that usually help
him. No use.'
  Fisher jabbered away into gibberish and I had to ask him to
speak more slowly. It seemed that Anton Bloomberg had
returned unexpectedly from Stockholm and soon after arriving at
the flat had suffered an asthmatic attack. It did not last long.
  'But soon after midnight it began again.'
  'Where are you?'
  'I'm here.'
  'Where's here?'
  'I'm at the flat, at the Bloombergs' flat. For Christ's sake,
come at once. *Please.*'
  Dressed, I went down to my surgery to pick up my leather
emergency bag. I kept thinking of what Fisher had said – that
Bloomberg had taken the ephedrine tablets I had prescribed for
him to abort an asthmatic attack but they had provided no relief.
I could see Yvonne's vandalised sacred face, observing her rough
and bawdy persecutor disadvantaged, in dire distress, and

waiting for me to ride in like a knight in shining armour, her loathed husband's saviour.

It seemed as if a stranger's venomous voice had been inserted in my brain: *Take the phial from the medicine cabinet*. It was a voice conversant with worms and epitaphs. And as I stood close to that medicine cabinet, hesitating, I considered the situation – not least the possible prolegomenon to the drama. What was Fisher doing at the Bloombergs' flat so late into the night? Bloomberg, he had said, had come back earlier than expected from Sweden. Vile imaginings. I turned away from the medicine chest.

Outside, I discovered it had been raining. My windscreen wipers brushed away the pattern of water on the glass as I drove fast through the deserted lamplit roads to the High Street. There the orange Belisha beacons blinked for no one. I passed the church before turning into a side road, steering the car between dark, slumbering houses. Soon I saw the block of flats ahead of me. I was surprised to see so many windows lit despite the hour.

Hugh Fisher opened the door for me and I followed him towards the spacious, elegant sitting room. 'Where's Yvonne?' I asked.

'She's in the bedroom. He doesn't want her near him. He doesn't want anybody near him.'

Bloomberg, his whole body heaving as he leant forward before an open window, was attempting desperately to breathe. I could hear the loud gasping wheeze of obstructed respiration. Bloomberg momentarily swivelled his head towards me revealing his sweating brow, the expanse of the white in his eyes, his open mouth, his cheeks cyanosed. Here was a face screaming. He could have been painted by Munch.

Hugh Fisher fidgeted near the door as I took the hypodermic syringe out of my bag. Correctly, I injected into my patient 4 minims of a 1 in 1000 solution of adrenaline. I remember that clearly and how afterwards I left the needle in. I did not withdraw it, but patiently waited every long thirty seconds while Bloomberg struggled before I injected a further minim. And so it went on and on and still Bloomberg experienced no relief.

I contemplated giving him a sedative. Sedatives are a useful adjunct in relieving severe asthma despite the danger of depressing respiratory function. Morphia, though, was to be avoided. That would demoralise the patient, lead to anoxia, leave the brain with too little oxygen, might even be fatal.

And then the door opened framing Yvonne, her eyes serious, searching mine. The frequent small doses of adrenaline that I was giving Bloomberg were having no effect. He still laboriously hungered for air. I withdrew the needle. I heard that venomous voice again, not my own, within my brain command me. 'Give that circumcised wretch, that tyrannous bully morphia, the sweetness of morphia, the sweet in the poison,' and now I hardly remember what happened next except that I must have obeyed that voice.

My own head seemed full of feathers. They both were standing there, Yvonne with her hand to her mouth and Hugh Fisher who seemed in a paralysed stupor. I remember yelling at him as I felt for the pulse of the unconscious Anton Bloomberg. I shouted again, 'Phone for an ambulance.' He needed hospital treatment, an oxygen tent. I'd given him a large dose of morphia, no doubt about it. Maybe at the hospital they would have the priceless cortisone to revive him. What have I done? Save him, Lord, and let foul be fair.

May 15th

I visited the hospital. Bloomberg is still in a coma and his respiration rate desperately slow. Yvonne sits beside his bed, waiting to see whether things might change or cease.

'Oh Robbie, whatever happens, happens,' she said to me quietly, so quietly, 'I know you did your best.'

Since I'm back home here now I've been pondering that whispered ambiguous remark. Was she hoping for his recovery or contemplating the freedom of widowhood? Most widows inhabit a darkened world but should Bloomberg die Yvonne would be like an escaped convict in summer sunlight.

The youthful registrar asked me how much morphia I had injected and how long it was before I had administered it. I told him less than the truth. Even so, I thought he was going to chide me. 'Treatment of status asthmaticus,' he said, loud enough for Yvonne to hear, 'is not easy to get right.' He glanced at Yvonne, seemingly in distress, pale and beautiful. 'As a last resort,' he said, 'a solution containing one-quarter grain of morphia, one hundredth of a grain of atropine and one in one thousand minims of adrenaline up to ten minims, to be injected every five minutes is permissible.'

I nodded. What else could I do? He was trying to show off his knowledge and expertise in front of an attractive woman. This was a trivial irritation. It was Bloomberg's condition that worried me. That worries me.

During my evening surgery I had to take blood from John Carter. I usually get into a vein quite easily, even in a case of myxoedema when the subcutaneous tissues everywhere are firm and podgy. But I observed my fingers trembling and I had to move from Carter's left arm to his right before I succeeded. During my clumsy performance I talked away cheerfully to John Carter. However depressed I felt within myself, I tried to remember how, when I was a student, the Dean at Westminster Hospital, Sir Adolphe Abrahams, used to say nasally, 'Don't forget, gentlemen, a man without a smiling face should not open a shop.' This evening I found it hard to fake one necessary smile. I must resolve not to greet my patients as if I were the doorman of a funeral parlour.

May 17th
I've been trying for the last two days to speak to Yvonne. When I telephone, Hugh Fisher answers, as if he were living there while Bloomberg is in hospital. Each time he says, 'She's taking

a rest, I'll get her to contact you when she wakes up,' or 'She's at the hospital,' or 'You've just missed her.'

Still Bloomberg breathes in and out, in and out in that hospital bed. His death bed?

It was such a labour this afternoon to get through my rounds. In the Finchley Road from my car I spotted Rachel Butler waiting at a bus stop. Now there's a widow who need not join Equity.

I never told Michael Butler he had an inoperable cancer. He did not ask me the awkward question. He knew what the verdict would be. Whenever I sense that patients do not care to talk about the diagnosis I do not consider it my duty to force the truth down their throats. Besides to tell the truth to patients is harder than to tell a lie.

After my last afternoon call I intended to visit the hospital again. I was too fatigued. I needed to go home and lie down for an hour or so.

As I write this I still feel inordinately tired. Tomorrow I must go to the hospital. I don't want to go to the hospital, to see the evidence of what I have done.

May 18th

In the middle of the night, I absurdly conjured up the idea that Hugh Fisher threatened to complain to the General Medical Council about my competence. Rhys reckoned that I should get in touch with the Medical Defence Union. Then I heard music. I got up. It seemed to be coming from next door. But the house next door is empty. The house next door is dark. I'm sure I heard music, not for long and only softly. Perhaps I am mistaken. I had taken a sedative. Maybe it was a side-effect of the drug? An auditory hallucination.

May 20th

Again Hugh Fisher answered the phone. He told me that Bloomberg had come out of the coma but the doctors had warned

Yvonne that because of his brain cells being deprived of oxygen the sequel would be serious.

'Brain damaged,' Hugh Fisher informed me.

'Can I speak to Yvonne?' I said.

'Er... just a minute.'

I held the receiver of the telephone, its inert material the same temperature as my hand. I pressed the thing to my ear as tightly as possible hoping I might hear some threads of conversation. I eavesdropped only on silence. At last, Hugh Fisher returned from the inaudible world and said, 'She must have just gone out.'

'Gone out?'

'Shopping, I think. We've no bread in the flat.'

'Right,' I said. 'Thank you.'

No bread in the flat. Evidently Fisher is sharing the apartment with Yvonne. Since that call I have experienced turbulent fantasies, some of which I'm too ashamed to recount here.

Tomorrow, or rather Monday, I shall ask Edith to cancel all my appointments from Wednesday on. And, after that, I shall get in a locum to see patients. Apart from fatigue, from time to time I feel too giddy as if I had Ménière's disease. I'm off balance.

May 23rd

At John Barnes I bumped into Mrs Levy. She had gone to a Broadhurst Gardens committee meeting. Hugh Fisher had told her about Anton Bloomberg's illness.

'I think he's a goner,' she said.

'I hear he's revived,' I countered.

'Really. His poor wife. They haven't been married a year. I don't hold with intermarriage but I do feel sorry for her.'

'I must be getting along,' I said.

'Ah, marriage,' she sighed. 'Well, you're a bachelor. That isn't healthy either, excuse me, doctor. You'd agree with Heine when he reckoned that the music at a wedding procession always reminded him of the music of soldiers going into battle.'

I smiled as I had to, nodded and began to move away but Mrs Levy clutched at my sleeve. 'Excuse me, doctor,' she repeated, 'but you don't look too well yourself.'

I sense that some external power is trying to implant ideas in my mind.

May 24th
If that cocky impossible registrar at the hospital has been critical, when speaking to Yvonne, of how I treated her husband – which seems to me likely – why should she shun me? Why should she behave as if that were the worst thing that could have occurred? Didn't she beg me to help her in an illicit way? True, not so drastically, but have I not acted as her friend, in her interest? I gave Anton Bloomberg too strong a dose. For a moment, I would have murdered for her.

May 27th
I forced myself to go to the hospital again and visit Anton Bloomberg only to discover that they sent him home on Friday. The registrar accosted me as I was walking down the corridor. 'Anoxia has left your patient irrevocably brain damaged,' he said – and he remarked on it so lightly as if he were commenting on the weather.

If I have been manipulated by Yvonne, then she shares my guilt. I gave that injection to Bloomberg while I was not myself, while I was sleep-walking. Mrs Gregorius was more honest than Yvonne. 'I must be straightforward with you,' she said to Dr Glas. 'Judge me as you will. I am an unfaithful wife. I belong to another man. And that's why it has become so terribly hard for me...'

On the other hand, I could be wrong. Hugh Fisher seems so...so asexual. I expect he's ambitious and hopes to take charge of the import-export business for Yvonne – just as Bloomberg did when her father, Tim Roberts, died. Perhaps it's only that: a necessary, though intimate, business relationship. After all, he always spoke well of Bloomberg. Would a wife's lover speak warmly of her husband? I don't know. I don't know and keep torturing myself.

At times I feel – I know it is a delusion – I feel Dr Glas is physically near to me. Those artfully arranged mirrors! When I walked to the borders of the Heath this afternoon at South End Green I felt he walked with me. When I picked up a small stone on the edge of the pond, I felt he threw it into the waters, and watched through my eyes the expanding ripples that made the ducks wobble. I am a stranger to myself.

Yvonne, I love you for what you are not.

May 31st

I've been in bed with a fever for the last three days. I must have picked up some sort of virus. I thought it might be an ear infection that made me feel intermittently giddy but Dr Andrews, who is taking my evening surgeries, examined my eardrums and told me that they are clear. He prescribed an antibiotic for me but I haven't taken it. I think it's a virus.

I phoned Yvonne yet again but Hugh Fisher answered. I told him I was unwell and confined to bed so would Yvonne please, please, telephone me.

She has not done so.

June 3rd

I'm so unsteady. I keep balance coming down the stairs holding on to the banister. In the living room I grasp a chair or the table. Edith has been very supportive. 'Don't worry about the afternoon rounds,' she said. 'If they're ill enough they'll come to Dr Andrews' evening surgery.' She contends that my locum looks like a gigolo. 'Still,' she said, 'he's adequate. But your patients love only you.' They are blind.

Though it has been a warm sunny day, after Edith left I built up a huge fire in the kitchen grate. I knew what I had to do. When, outside, the sun reluctantly sank down in its colourful flamingo-funeral pomp behind the rooftops and the swifts could no longer be seen mating on the wing, I climbed the stairs to my study and brought down the book, *Doctor Glas*, that Yvonne Bloomberg had given me, that has so haunted me. The fire I had fed with coal and logs would be its crematorium incinerator. It would be a kind of exorcism.

I felt impelled to wait until it was dark, until I could see, through the window, the first star appear. I did not put the light on in the kitchen. The log fire provided enough illumination. As in murder, as in making love, little light was needed. The sunset that had ignited the windows of the houses earlier now seemed to reside, in part, in the firegrate. The flames there had been unlocked. I heard the spit and the crack of the sparks flying. The fire was so hungry. I put on yet another log. It became even wilder as I delivered Dr Glas to its incandescent heart.

The book fell open as if clamouring to be read. At first it did not catch alight. I thrust the poker at it violently and I felt a momentary exultation as the flames took hold to gradually devour the blackening pages. With the tall flowers of fire the chimney roared as if it knew somebody was being sacrificed. I watched figures form and proliferate in the dance of the flames. I saw a mask-like face. It must have been that of Dr Glas. He was burning, burning as if he were a Guy Fawkes scarecrow. I could not help touch my own face. The skin was warm from the flames.

Fire's a strange thing. It has to kill to live. It's true of man too, is it not? Afterwards I wanted to cry. No tears. I cried without tears. Ash.

June 4th

I could not concentrate well enough to play chess with Rhys. I put him off. I think he was glad. He was free to go to Richmond.

In the afternoon I took a sedative because thoughts kept racing through my head, thoughts about Yvonne, about Fisher and Bloomberg, about Charlie and Rhys – all sorts of memory thoughts about people and things. It seemed appropriate that suddenly the horn of a parked car outside started for no reason and would not stop.

In my dreams I take the road to Nowhere.

June 5th

I, cloud-watching, took a deckchair into the garden this afternoon. I sat there for hours. When, at one point, I happened to open my mouth, I saw a white butterfly, one unused to flying it seemed, new, stagger in front of my face – as if it had come out of my mouth! I watched it float, rise and fall and lift crookedly across the bushes over the obstacle of the cob-webbed wall into the garden of the empty house next door. My soul has left my body. I am empty.

June 6th

All day I've felt unwell as if I had the liver of a blaspheming Jew. Then I came across the *Dr Glas* book that Charlie Forster had given me. I had forgotten about it. To the fire, to the fire with it.

June 7th

I have written my will. Who would have thought I had kept the cyanide for myself? Each wakeful night now I keep the phial on the little table next to my bed, (symbolically) close to the small alarm clock. If I have the courage to take it this house and all its furniture will be bequeathed to Edith. All my money and investments will go to that new organisation Oxfam, started in Oxford by the Quakers. All the paintings and books to my friend, Rhys. My mother's jewellery (still in her bedroom) to my cousin, Marjorie. And this journal to YVONNE BLOOMBERG, Bitch.

So, tonight or the next night or the night after. It is my fate.

June 8th

I cannot sleep. It's hopeless. Such a heat wave. Earlier I thought of going out though it was after midnight. To go out into the deserted streets and walk on and on. Or take a night swim in the Hampstead Heath pond, the one with the raft in it. I would have discovered other insomniacs around the periphery of the pond. Utterly silent, they fish in the darkness.

Now, at this open window, I breathe in the night odour of honeysuckle. Strange – for a moment I thought I saw a light in the empty house next door. As if someone moved about inside carrying a lit candle. But the house now is dark like the one that the angelic young girl went into in Netherhall Gardens. I stare at the phial on the bedside table. I haven't the courage.

June 9th

Another hot, stifling night. I write this sitting before the open window. Intermittently I hear someone shouting in the unlit house next door. I cannot hear him quite. Just then he yelled, 'Mine.' Or it could have been, 'Swine.' Who is he shouting at? If he would shout louder I could report exactly what he is saying. Now he is quiet.

It's 2 a.m. already, dammit. I didn't sleep a wink last night and I'm alert now, too alert. The weather doesn't help: it's so sultry. It might thunder soon. Thunder has been forecast. Meanwhile I bet that in the hospital one of the big lifts is empty, brightly lit. I know its doors will open and shut at each floor, at each deserted corridor. No one will come out. No one will go in. It is a slave of its bleak mechanism. All night it will go up and down, up and down the black shaft.

He's started to shout again. For a few seconds only. In German, I think.

A small thud as if he had thrown a mass of wet confetti at the wall.

I feel so low.

I telephoned Charlie. He helped me once. Maybe, somehow, he could help me again? But when I heard his voice irritably saying, 'Hello, hello,' I could not speak. My phone call had woken him up. I put the receiver down.

A thought: just as fire has to kill to live, so the masochistic candle bestows the gift of a gentle light by destroying itself.

June 10th
It is June 10th. My father's birthday. Each night my hand wants to go to the phial like filings drawn to a magnet. No.

June 11th
Once more I slept for only three or four hours last night. How odd to dream of a photograph, a photo of Chekhov's study, the one I'd found in my mother's snapshot album. The photo became real! A door opened and in came a shadowy figure, a man who sat with his back to me at Chekhov's desk. Was this Anton Chekhov himself? Or the timber merchant who had probably sent the photograph to my mother? The man was bending over to write something in a diary. I turned away but suddenly I knew with absolute certainty that the man at the desk was Dr Glas. And writing in my diary! I looked again – the chair was empty.

June 12th
I am on the rack.
   I know nothing and have forgotten everything.
   I am searching, mother, for my bride.

PART THREE

10 Crusoe Road,
London NW3
January 20th 2000

Dear Simon,

Thank you for our delightful lunch at the Plurabelle. Since then I have followed your suggestion and interviewed Yvonne Bloomberg again. On this occasion her stricken husband and her partner, Hugh Fisher, were in attendance. I have been reassured that – to use Mrs Bloomberg's words – 'Dr Charles Forster and his colleagues are, at present, settling their accounts in hell and Mrs Amy Middleton joined them in that centrally-heated place last October.' So, as far as I can see, there is no danger of any libel concerns.

That Amy Middleton only passed away in 1999 appears to be one reason why Mrs Bloomberg held back for so many years before offering the Dr Simmonds journals for publication. Hugh Fisher was also obstructive until now. Indeed, Yvonne Bloomberg would have liked to add a postscript to the book in which she would refute many of the value judgements made about herself and her partner but I have persuaded her otherwise. As they say, confession is a medicine for those who have gone astray.

When Sam Cohen returns from the USA I trust he will read the journals swiftly and you and he will let us have your decision soon.

Yours sincerely,
Peter Dawson

DANNIE ABSE

10 Crusoe Road,
London NW3
January 20th 2000

Dear Yvonne,

Just a note to let you know that the project is still very much alive. Their chief editor is away at present but Simon Gower has recommended *The Journals of Dr Simmonds* strongly. So, fingers crossed.

I'm trying, at present, to find a copy of the Swedish novel. I'm curious to read it. Presumably you came upon it in translation. Dr Simmonds's quotes from the book are in English. Do you happen to know when the English language edition was published and by whom?

Best wishes,
Peter

10 Crusoe Road,
London NW3
February 17th 2000

Dear Simon,

I'm so pleased Sam Cohen has taken to the Journals but I can't agree with him that Robert Simmonds was anti-semitic and that this might preclude a possible American edition. I asked Yvonne Bloomberg if she believed Dr Simmonds held anti-semitic views and she replied drily, 'No, I don't think so – at least not much more than most!'

As for changing the title – by all means. The book must be presented as a novel and I concur with Sam Cohen when he remarks that the title *The Journals of Dr Simmonds* is open to misinterpretation and might find itself on the non-fiction shelves of Waterstone's.

I have procured a copy of *Doctor Glas* and have read it with admiration – an English edition. So, for the few quotes in our book acknowledgements should be made to the able translator, Paul Britten Austin. As you know, Hjalmar Söderberg's novel was published in Sweden in 1905 and attained the status of a contemporary classic. I wonder if, following the publication of Dr Simmonds's journals, you would consider reprinting *Doctor Glas* as translated by P.B. Austin. It is intriguing to compare the books – and readers might be interested to do that, especially if our book sells well. I fully agree with William Sansom when he, no mean author himself, enthused about the 1905 novel of Söderberg and wrote in 1963, 'In most of its writing and much of the frankness of its thought, it might have been written tomorrow...'

Well, tomorrow is today!

Yours sincerely,
Peter Dawson

10 Crusoe Road,
London NW3
March 17th 2000

Dear Yvonne,

I have pleasure in sending you two contracts. Please sign both, keep one, and return the other to me. The title *Dr Simmonds and Dr Glas* is provisional.

I'm glad that it has all worked out.

Best wishes,
Peter

10 Crusoe Road,
London NW3
March 23rd 2000

Dear Yvonne,

I'm taken aback that you wish to withdraw the manuscript at this late stage. I understand your ambivalence about inviting strangers to judge your part in the tragedy. Of course you are not responsible for Dr Simmonds's incompetent, indeed criminal, performance that night in May 1950, nor for his immoderate infatuation with you. And how could you guess that he would have such an obsession with the book you gave him? I understand, too, that you would wish to correct his warped view of your earlier relationship with your present partner. Even so, I would urge you to sign the contracts. Let us discuss it.

Look, may I call on you this coming week-end? I shall telephone you to arrange a suitable time.

Best wishes,
Peter

10 Crusoe Road,
London NW3
March 28th 2000

Dear Simon,

With regard to your query about *Dr Glas* and American rights. Yes, it was published in the USA as an *Atlantic Monthly* book in 1963. My guess is that it has long been out of print though a film was made of it, directed by Mai Zetterling.

You may be interested to know that I had to call on Yvonne Bloomberg last weekend. She suddenly had doubts about making Dr Simmonds's journals public so, armed with a large bunch of white tulips, I managed to reassure her. I was helped, too, by Hugh Fisher who is keen for the publication to go ahead as he hopes that, with some of the advance money, Yvonne would let him buy a seventeenth century map of Hyrcarnia. 'Not a chance,' Yvonne Bloomberg whispered to me afterwards, 'we have too many debts.'

Hyrcarnia? Apparently it was a province of ancient Asia along the Caspian Sea. Fisher told me excitedly that in *Henry VI* Shakespeare refers to the 'tigers of Hyrcania'. Well, wouldn't you know?

Tortoise-paced Anton Bloomberg hardly says anything. Just smiles inanely. From Dr Simmonds's description of him you would think he had a visage that would deter a ravenous cannibal. Age and illness hardly beautify features but I would have thought that the younger Bloomberg would have been presentable enough. Yvonne treats him and Hugh Fisher with patient concern as if they were both her children. At one point Anton Bloomberg began to eat the tulips I had brought. I pretended not to notice until Yvonne shouted, 'Stop that, dear.'

Last weekend I also saw Tim Howells who, at present, is represented by Drew and Davidson. He is dissatisfied with them and hinted he would like to change agents. He is close to finishing another novel. I could, I think, deliver him and it to you. Interested?

Best regards,
Peter

Acknowledgements:
To my brother, Wilfred, who, more than thirty years ago gave me Hjalmar Söderberg's classic Swedish novel, *Doctor Glas*, originally published in 1905.

To Chatto and Windus for quotations taken from the English language version of *Doctor Glas* translated by Paul Britten Austin.

To my wife, Joan, for her generous encouragement and her invaluable editorial skills.

D.A.